MW01613875

SHADE

A STORY OF THE LEGACY

R.G. ROBERTS

Copyright © 2021 by R.G. Roberts

All rights reserved.

No part of this publication may be reproduced, distributed, or transmitted in any form or by any means, including photocopying, recording, or other electronic or mechanical methods, without the prior written permission of the publisher, except as permitted by U.S. copyright law. For permission requests, contact [include publisher/author contact info].

The story, all names, characters, and incidents portrayed in this production are fictitious. No identification with actual persons (living or deceased), places, buildings, and products is intended or should be inferred.

Book Cover by Deranged Doctor Designs

3rd edition, 2022

*To Shira. Without you, I never would have gotten this story
off the ground.*

CONTENTS

1

FREEDOM

Olorian army slaves were some of the worst treated slaves in Evendar.

Not that the Olorian army was a disciplined lot with sophisticated needs. Rather the opposite; the Olorians depended on Evendarian slaves for most of their organization, cooking, cleaning, and day-to-day care. Evendarian slaves, who were kept chained in leaky barracks at night, made beds, bread and basically saw to the army's every need during the day.

Those same slaves were beaten and abused—frequently worked to death because they were one of the cheapest commodities in Evendar. You could always grab another one.

Slaves were cheaper than horses, too, which was why ten of them pulled one cart while teams of disgruntled horses hauled the other three. The guards mostly ignored them, save for yelling or applying the whip when one staggered, or another slowed. After all, the slaves were chained to the cart. Where were they going to go?

The sixteen slaves attached to the backs of the other carts—presumably slaves with specific skill sets who the overseer didn't want to exhaust before nightfall—were a little better off. But they were still shackled by the wrists, with four attached to each cart. They walked with their heads down and didn't speak, flinching when one of the guards or the overseers on the wagons glanced their way.

Seven soldiers, four overseers. The latter were armed with whips and daggers, but not swords. The guards wore the typical Olorian falcata-style sword at their belt, but none wore armor. Their eyes focused inwards, too, not looking for external threats.

If they had been, they might've noticed a lone rider just beyond the tree line, cloaked and watching them. Like the slaves, he was Evendarian.

Unlike them, he was armed.

Shade counted the guards and overseers again, noting the way the two guards in the back laughed and passed a flask between them. All the guards were mounted, which increased the chance of one of them getting away, even if the rear pair was drunk. Which they were.

Silently, Shade freed a sling from his saddlebags. The sling was at least two decades old, made for an army that no longer existed. The long, braided cords were made from flax, and the diamond-shaped pouch between them was weather-beaten leather, formed by time and used to be a perfect cradle for rounded stones.

Shade slipped the loop over his index finger and loaded the sling with an almond-shaped sling bullet without looking. Once he had the sling in his right hand, he left it dangling and nudged his horse forward with his legs. Slinging from horseback was not the old Evendarian army tradition—accuracy was hard, and it took a well-trained mount—but it was a skill Shade perfected long ago, in another life.

The slave chain was past him now, trudging along the Via Indus towards New Allus. The Via Indus was one of the oldest roads in Evendar, starting down in South Sarin, winding across the Bridge before twisting west to the Ardens Mountains.

Fredi vasGollep's army camp lay further along that road, Shade knew. It was deep in the Sunder River Valley and undoubtedly the final destination for this slave chain. New Allus, however, was a fishing town, which explained the empty barrels on the carts.

Drunken laughter drifted back to Shade as he guided his horse onto the road. The back two guards were shit soldiers, still sharing that flask. The middle pairs half-watched the slaves as they chatted with the overseers. The officer out front—Shade guessed she was an officer based on her nicer clothes because the Olorian army wasn't big on uniforms or uniformity— pointedly ignored the rest of them.

Her funeral.

Whipping his arm up and around, Shade released the bullet at the bottom of the arc. It sped through the air without even a whistle, striking the rear right guard in the back of the head with a wet *plop*. He crumbled out of the saddle without ever knowing what hit him.

By the time his companion twisted around, Shade had already reloaded. His arm snapped around again, and another almond-shaped rock arced out, hitting this guard in the left eye and driving straight into his brain. He never had a chance to scream, collapsing like a sail without wind.

Shade didn't watch him hit the ground. Instead, he reloaded two more times, taking out the two guards on the left. One took the stone through an eye, and another straight through the throat; both fell from the saddle as bloody messes.

Four down, three to go. One overseer screeched in terror; Shade ignored him, looped the sling around his saddle's pommel, and drew his sword. Left hand back on the reins, he urged his stallion forward to meet the two righthand guards.

The first was braver or more foolish than the other; she came at Shade with a shouted war cry, her falcata held high. He parried, riposted, and stabbed her in the heart. The second came at him a moment later, but he was left-handed and on the wrong side for his sword to reach Shade. He tried twisting in the saddle, but Shade was quicker. A soft kiss from his schiavona opened the Olorian's throat from right to left.

That left the officer, who was trying to rally the overseers. One was stupid enough to dismount from his wagon and approach Shade, waving his dagger. A fast downward stab sent him to his maker; Shade didn't bother to watch him fall.

The officer hesitated too long, pausing in front of the chained-up slaves behind the second cart. With a cry, two of them dragged her out of the saddle, burying her beneath a rain of punches and kicks as she tried to fight. She screamed in fury, but they kept her down, kicking her sword away when she tried to draw it.

The back left slave grabbed for the officer's falcata, snarling as she raised it over her head. The blade came down; blood splashed up.

Shade nodded approvingly. Slaves didn't always fight back.

The remaining overseers, eyes wide, jumped off their wagons and fled. Sheathing his sword, Shade freed the sling again, reloading and whipping it around.

One strike.

Two.

Neither overseer made it to the tree line.

Movement caught Shade's eye—there were riders coming up the road. But these rode two by two and wore armor—*Evendarian* armor? What kind of fools rode about like some sort of old-style militia, advertising the very weapons that the Olorians made illegal to wear?

Aging and worn down though he might be, Shade's eyes still worked fine. Those riders wore schiavonas.

Sighing, Shade stowed his sling and dismounted. He'd deal with the imbeciles when they arrived. For now, he crouched and pulled a ring of keys off the dead overseer's belt.

A few strides carried him to the closest quartet of slaves and the cart they were chained behind. They watched him warily but didn't draw back, meekly offering their wrists to be unchained.

"Who are you?" one whispered. She was a young woman, maybe fifteen, beautiful beneath the dirt and bruises on her face. Her hair was burgundy, and her eyes dark gray.

"My name is Shade."

"You're a Night Rider?" the man next to her said, "I've heard of Night Riders!"

The young woman frowned. "What are Night Riders?"

"They help people." He beamed.

2

UNWORTHY

S hade pushed back the urge to grimace. "Unlock your compatriots."

The woman took the keys from him, pulling another of the now-former slaves along, a boy who resembled her enough to be her brother.

"My name is Gwaun," the eager man said. He was a typical Evendarian in looks— brown-haired, brown-eyed, and lanky.

"So it is." Shade checked to see if the Olorian officer was breathing when Gwaun and his silent companion stepped away. She wasn't. "Help the others."

"What can I do?" Gwaun asked.

Stop talking to me, Shade thought. He wanted to say it, but even at his worst, he wasn't that ill-mannered. His eyes flicked to the riders approaching. They didn't wear uniforms— Lady help them, at least they weren't that stupid— but they were in something approaching a military formation. There were eighteen of the fools, though.

Gwaun followed his gaze. "Are they Night Riders, too?"

"No."

"But they're not Olorians, right? I mean, you just killed a bunch—I mean nine of them, but that's a lot more. Could you do that?" Gwaun barely paused for breath, his voice rising in pitch with each word. "Are they coming to take us back?"

"That's not happening." Shade turned back to Gwaun, resisting the urge to scare him into silence. Pity that murdering someone he'd just saved was bad form. "Whoever they are, they're Evendarians. And you're going to Median."

"Median?" Gwaun squeaked.

"There are people who will help you there."

"There are?"

Shade gritted his teeth until his jaw hurt; it didn't take long. "Yes."

Median was one of the northern towns that had a tacit agreement with the Night Riders: help people brought there, and Night Riders would continue to help them. Median was a big town, big enough for former slaves to get lost in. It was also one of many towns in the densely populated area at the top of the Bridge, which meant those needing to avoid Olorian eyes could shuffle between them and never be found.

"Thank you!" Gwaun's eyes whipped wildly between Shade and the approaching riders. "I should've said that before."

"There's no need to thank me." Shade loosened his sword in the scabbard, regretting putting her away with blood on the blade. "Now, step back."

"Do you think these people will—"

"Be silent."

Gwaun's mouth snapped shut with an audible *click*.

Shade sidestepped away from him when Gwaun didn't back away fast enough. The other former

8

slaves were smarter, gathering around the woman who unchained them, well away from any potential confrontation. *She* was the smart one. Shade wondered if he could dump Gwaun on her and leave her in charge.

Slowing their horses to a trot, the riders fanned out, so they were four abreast on the road. The group stopped about twenty feet away from Shade and the ruins of the slave chain. Their leader cut that distance in half before stopping his horse.

"You are a Night Rider?" he asked.

"I'm not sure I like your tone." Shade *didn't* like this situation. Twenty-two innocents at his back and eighteen potential hostiles was a recipe for death and doom.

The leader scoffed. He was definitely Evendarian, with aquiline features and blond hair. His accent tried to be imperial, too, with the sharpness the capital city's old merchant class affected when they pretended to be noble. It took a good ear to notice the differences.

"You are under arrest for rebellion, murder, and treason against the queen," the leader said. "You will disarm and come with us."

"Treason against the *queen?*" Shade laughed. "What queen would that be?"

The leader rolled his eyes. "You know we mean Queen Nydein. If you—"

"The Queen of Olor is no queen of mine." The words felt like ash in his mouth.

Just thinking of Olor's queen, of the woman who conquered his country, enslaved his people, and killed his king, left Shade cold.

"Whether or not you acknowledge her, she rules. If you surrender quietly, we will take these people onto Median and safety."

"How kind of you, offering to help your own people with conditions attached." Shade snorted. "If I didn't know better, I might've taken you for Olorians."

The leader reared back as if slapped. "We're better than that. We're *venatores*, in service of the state."

"In service of *Olor*, you mean." Shade's eyes narrowed. "*Venatores* served Evendar. Not the brutes who call themselves our masters. You're not worthy to yourself *venatores*."

"You cannot fight all of us. Put down your sword."

Shade drew his schiavona. He figured that was answer enough.

"Fine. You're worth less dead, but—" The leader cut off, staring. "What are you doing?"

Feet shuffled against the stone. Shade sensed them moving before he snuck a glance over his shoulder to see the former slaves moving to support him. Most held weapons they'd pulled off the dead Olorians, swords and daggers in the main, but one held a bow in shaking hands.

"Our fight is not with you." The leader's eyes darted back and forth, taking in the glaring group. "We wish you no harm."

"Yeah, but you want to kill the man who just saved us," Gwaun said. "Or hand him to Olor. That doesn't seem right. We know what they do to people who fight."

Shade blinked. He wasn't used to people he saved being willing to fight. As Gwaun said, Olor usually beat it right out of them all too quickly.

He opened his mouth to argue, to tell them *he* should protect *them*—and then shut it. Who was he to tell Evendarians not to fight for what they believed in?

A strange and warm feeling stole into his chest, just for a moment. Something like hope.

"You'll have to go through us, too." The red-haired woman pushed forward to stand next to Gwaun.

"We're not here to hurt you," the leader said. "We're Evendarians."

She stuck her chin out. "So's he."

"You tell them, Cara," her brother muttered.

"*He* has broken Olorian laws and—"

"By saving people like us?" It was Gwaun again, bubbling forward. "Yeah, that seems terrible." His laugh was a squeak, but damn, the boy was trying to be brave. "I may not know a lot— it's hard to get a lot of news when you're stuck as an Olorian army slave— but none of us are dumb."

Redness crept up the *venator* leader's cheeks like a creeping tide; Shade stepped forward before the man could snap out an order that might doom these plucky fools.

"I'm taking these people to safety." Shade smiled coldly. "Feel free to try and take me afterward if you want."

The lead *venator* looked from Shade to the others and then back to Shade again. "This isn't over."

"Oh, I'm sure it isn't."

Median was a two-day journey away at a plodding cart horse's pace. Even with the former slaves riding on the carts in place of the empty barrels, they made terrible time. Shade kept his distance from the group, riding ahead as often as possible, mostly to escape Gwaun's constant jabbering. Fortunately, Cara— who was much quieter— took charge of her fellows and seemed to sense that Shade preferred little to no conversation.

It wasn't that he didn't *care* for them. Shade made sure they were protected, fed, and bandaged wounds as required. He just didn't like crowds of people, particularly ones determined to mob him with gratitude.

The *venatores* lurked miles behind. Sometimes, Shade spotted their advance scouts; others, they fell out of sight.

"I'll leave you here," he said to Cara when Median became visible on the horizon. "Go to the Blue Horse. The *hospitia* owner is Rhona Mus. She'll help you find safe places."

Cara smiled tightly, sitting close to her brother on the driver's seat of the lead cart. "You need to get a jump on them, don't you?"

"It will make things easier."

Never mind that he'd intended to buy supplies and rest his horse in Median. That option was off the table, now. Shade had enough jerky and cheese to last a few days, though, as well as a loaf of bread that wasn't quite hard. He'd survive.

"Thank you for everything," Cara said. "We owe you our lives."

"Rhona knows a healer who can get rid of your brands. Talk to her."

"We will. Thank you again."

He wished she'd stop saying that. Shade inclined his head. "Be safe."

"And you."

Wheeling his horse around, Shade rode away from the repurposed slave chain without looking back. The *venatores* had drifted out of sight again. Now was the best time to give them the slip. If Fortuna smiled upon him, Shade might slip right around the *venatores,* ride south and lose them.

If not...things would get messy.

3

— • —

SILENCE

H e was grateful for the silence.

Silence was safety for a Night Rider. Silence and darkness were his best shields, particularly with trappers on his tail. Any competent Night Rider could disappear into the darkness like a whispered prayer. Those who couldn't rarely survived.

Shade was a survivor.

He rose quietly, letting his eyes adjust to the darkness. The forest was quiet; this early, even the homeless who fled into the wilderness still slept. And he'd made camp far from them, more for their sake than his.

The one thing he hated about the silence was that it gave him space to think. Space to think about a time when his world had not always been so, of a time when outlaws who kept to shadows were not Evendar's last and best hope. Conquest by their old enemy left his nation broken...and led those who would fight for her, those like Shade, to become Night Riders.

His horse, who he'd named Victrix—it meant "Victory" in the old tongue—in a rare bout of optimism, stood tethered to the right. The stallion was a dappled gray, his color fading as he aged, but currently, just the right color to fade into the early morning. Vic slept quietly, with his saddle straddling a downed tree by his side.

The remnants of his small fire were only a mess of ash. No Night Rider was fool enough to leave a fire burning when closing their eyes for the night. Darkness meant safety.

The *venatores* were out there somewhere, perhaps a mile distant. No more than two. He'd not lost them, not yet. He'd probably need another day's ride before he could hope to. But he was too experienced to panic. This was not the first time he found himself as a hunting party's prey.

Clucking his tongue softly, he woke Vic. The horse, accustomed to this business, shook his head to chase the sleep away, gracefully accepting both saddle and bridle after a quick once-over with a brush. The stallion nickered softly, butting him once in the shoulder with a velvety nose. For a moment, he allowed his forehead to rest upon the dapple-gray neck.

In this life of hiding and running, Vic was his only companion. Together, they lost many a trapper and defeated many an enemy. Today, they'd do that again. An early start would help. His pursers would surely rise with the sun. They were young and probably thought that meant getting up early.

They were also young enough to think they could trade sleep for numbers and remounts. Perhaps they'd be right. Employed by Olorians as they were, could they simply *take* horses if none were offered? A Night Rider couldn't—and wouldn't. At least not from Evendarians.

Besides, outright thievery was a stupid option when it meant trading in an excellent horse for a mediocre one. But those following him didn't quite understand that; they assumed outnumbering him and moving faster would give them every advantage they needed.

A bird sang softly in the trees above him; another answered from further away, towards the road. The air smelled of rain and storms. Good. Those would hide his tracks.

"Ready?" he asked Vic.

His fellow Night Riders said Shade talked to his horse more than he did people. They were probably right. Vic would not share his secrets.

And Vic didn't blabber until Shade's head hurt, either.

Vic butted his head into Shade's hip. He scratched the horse's neck, secured his saddlebags, and then swung his leg over the stallion's back. It was time to move.

He might only have a couple of hours' head start, but with that came a lead he could build up during the day. He could lose them by backtracking and crisscrossing over his own trail before it grew cold. The *venatores* were excellent trackers, better than usual. They'd stayed with him since Median when he thought he might lose them on the first day. But Shade still had a few tricks left to try.

Still, he wished they were not his countrymen.

Olorians were easy to lead on a merry chase. Most of them had shoddy discipline and little to no training. It was almost easy. They rarely tailed him for more than a few hours, even when they hunted in packs and bragged that they would bring home a Night Rider's head.

He'd also kill Olorians, if not happily, at least easily. While the danger of being caught was no less—torture and death, or worse—Shade did not fear them.

He knew Olorian tactics; he could lose them in his sleep.

Not the *venatores*. They'd chased him for two days already, losing more than half their number in the process when they split up to cover three possible trails. But the last of them kept up annoyingly well. Under other circumstances, Shade might've set up an ambush and picked a few of them off—or even killed the lot of them—but these were men of Evendar.

His people.

The *gall* of them choosing to call themselves *venatores* still rankled. Just thinking of that title made Shade go cold. Once, years ago, *venatores* had been state-sponsored trappers who hunted criminals. Back before the Evendarian Empire died. Now, these men worked for Olor.

They were willing to turn their weapons on their own instead of against the invaders, betraying everything Evendar once stood for—and hunting the *only* people who still fought for Evendar's people.

So far as Shade knew, he was their first target.

The irony was thick enough to make him laugh. The first Night Rider to be hunted by his fellow Evendarians was the *first* Night Rider. Did they know? Most only knew him by the name he'd chosen. Even among the Night Riders, rumors swirled about his background; even most of the old timers didn't know.

Shade didn't bother telling the younger Night Riders he started their outlaw-born revolution. He laughed to himself when some told stories about how there'd been many men called Shade and how a new man took on the mantle every time the last was killed. The legends were useful...even if they brought him to this.

A touch of his heels sent Vic trotting away from their campsite. Shade left nothing behind to identify himself, only ashes. The *venatores*—oh, he would have to learn to think that name without letting his blood boil—would probably find it. If so, they'd learn nothing. Shade would be far away by dawn.

Vic pulled at the reins, eager to be off and run free. Shade kept a firm hold on him until they found the forest road. Traveling along the main road was dangerous, but good footing saved time and left less of a trail to follow. It was also smarter in the dark. Vic tripping and falling could kill them both.

At first light, he'd abandon the road and travel cross-country, but for now, Shade would stick with the ancient Via Indus, named for a once-great king of a fallen nation. This road, like so much around him, was one more reminder of all the world lost in the Fall.

The Olorians could conquer, but they built no new civilization to replace what was lost. Instead, they enslaved Evendarians and made merry upon the ruins.

Scowling, he allowed an inch of rein to slip through his fingers, giving Vic his head for a bit. The spirited stallion would be easier to handle once he had his fun.

And the wind upon his face might make him forget, even if only for a little while.

4

INSTANCE

Two nights later, Shade rode into a small town, tired to the bone but certain he finally slipped out of the net. He'd not seen the trappers for forty-three hours nor slept during that time, but he was finally free of the chase. It was time for good food and a proper bed, perhaps even a bath, to clean off the grime. Despite the years he spent on the road, he'd never grown used to feeling dirty.

Yes, a bath would be nice. Shade felt like he had three weeks of dirt caked under his nails and in unmentionable places.

Maybe there'd even be hot water.

Wordlessly, he dismounted and tossed the stable boy a quartet of brozen sestertii for his trouble. The kid's eyes widened, and Shade gave him a nod before moving toward the *hospitia* door. Generally, Vic was more mischievous than friendly, but after two long days on the road, he got touchy.

It wouldn't do for Vic to bite the boy, which he'd do if the boy tried to muscle him around. That'd probably make the kid kick the horse, and then Vic would trample him. With money in his pocket, the boy would be more indulgent and probably wouldn't

21

get bitten in the first place. And then Shade wouldn't have to deal with irate parents or employers, either.

Striding out of the barn, warm wind kissed his cheeks. It was unusually warm for fall, even here near the equator. But it also smelled like rain was coming; the storm clouds on the horizon were closing in fast. A good time to stop.

Habit brought Shade's right hand up to pull the hood up of his dark gray cloak as his left reached for the *hospitia*'s worn door. Keeping his sword hand free was as necessary as pulling up the hood was in this business. Even if most people couldn't tell two Night Riders apart, anonymity had its advantages. He wanted rest tonight, not a fight with some idiot hoping to earn the price off his head.

The *hospitia*'s interior was musty but cheerily enough lighted in the areas most of the patrons frequented. The back left corner was darker, however, with just one lamp; just how Night Riders liked it.

Weltil was once a large and thriving town at the eastern foot of the Bridge, the narrow strip of land connecting the continents of North and South Sarin. However, invading Olorian armies rampaged through after the Battle of the Bridge. After the last of the great army of Evendar fell and the tide turned, Weltil was pillaged, raped, and burned.

Overnight, the town transformed from a prosperous trading city to a ghost town. Little was rebuilt since then. The citizens not sold into slavery sought their new beginnings elsewhere, some running north to the mountains or the small, independent nations as yet outside Olorian grasp. Only the hardiest and most dedicated remained.

Olorians moved into half of the remaining structures, at least for a while. After a few years, most of them drifted west to Bridgetown, which was larger, and poor Evendarians trickled back in when the Olorians left. Most didn't have money to rebuild, so they cobbled together what they could, frequently building one house out of the remnants of two.

The tragedy of Weltil made it an appropriate place for Night Riders to meet. They, too, were relics of a bygone age. The chance of finding at least one Night Rider on any night in Gunstrum's *Hospitia* was high. You'd always find them at the same table, sitting with their back against the wall, hooded and cloaked, eyes missing nothing.

Gunstrum's was a large hotel, a holdover from when Weltil was bigger and safer. The building was a tall, four-story inn and tavern, with guest rooms stacked over the ground floor dining room. It wasn't a high-end *hospitia*—before the war, the rich would've shunned it as low class—lacking a garden or formal atrium. It did have a central bar area, with a u-shaped marble bar and a large dining area, but the two were separated by pillars instead of the wall a nicer establishment would have.

Still, Gunstrum's was *safe*. Or what passed for safe for Night Riders on the road. That was hard to find these days, particularly with their own countrymen hunting them.

That thought still left Shade angry enough to make nausea churn in his gut.

He paused at the bar, his eyes flicking right. There was someone at the table already, a silhouette he recognized by the way one shoulder sat higher than the other. Shade laid a coin upon the stained and sanded bar.

"Ale." He nodded to the approaching bartender.

It was a busy night. Gunstrum was tending the bar himself. To the right, in the dining area, patrons clumped together, laughing and eating, with nary an Olorian in sight. A group around one round table played dice; another pair arm-wrestled. Something twisted in Shade's chest before he forced himself to look away.

Focus. He was too tired for this.

Food, drink, and then that bath. Maybe then he could sleep. Gunstrum's had a bathing area, usually with hot water. That sounded something like paradise.

There was a storm brewing outside, and inclement weather always made for good business, especially at either end of the Bridge. *No one* wanted to be out there during a powerful storm, even a Night Rider. Parts of the Bridge causeway, weathered and neglected since the fall of the Empire, were halfway underwater even during dry months, now.

Years ago, there were breakwaters built into both sides of the Bridge, but those fell into disrepair after a major battle and Olorian neglect. If the season was wet, as this summer was, fording your way across the narrower parts of the Bridge was common.

"No wine?" Gunstrum cocked his head, speaking up to be heard over the crowd. "I've got your favorite."

"Not tonight." Shade shook his head.

Two years ago, the *hospitia* keeper's youngest daughter was accosted by a gang of ruffians who hauled her off to an Olorian slave market when they finished with her. After Gunstrom gave her up for lost—having no choice, lest he end up in a slave

24

market himself—Shade stumbled upon her when wrecking said slave market, then brought her home.

He refused payment, as he always did. Ever since Gunstrum paid particular care of the man who he called King of the Road and tried to keep a bottle of his favorite in reserve. Tonight, however, was not an evening for relaxation.

"I won't accept payment from you, you know." Gunstrum slid him a mug of house ale and crossed his arms.

"Take it anyway." He left the coin on the bar. "The Olorian I took it from has no further need of money." That one was a rapist. Shade couldn't get them all, but he'd never regret removing that particular head from its assigned set of shoulders.

Ignoring Gunstrom's protest, Shade walked to the table in the dark corner, setting his mug down and sliding into the chair across from his compatriot.

"Shade." The other man's voice was soft.

"Instance." Shade sipped his ale. It was surprisingly good.

Instance was a short and stocky man with graying red hair and bright green eyes. Once, those eyes were framed by laugh lines and freckles. Now, the lines were etched in by age and hardship, and the smiles were more rare.

Greetings between Night Riders never included true names, not even between old friends. It wasn't worth the risk. If the Olorians knew who you were, they'd go after your family—and kill everyone.

Or worse.

"What brings you this way? I thought you were further north. Reckoning said he saw you up by New Lotell." Instance fiddled with his sleeve, shoving it out of the way to scratch his arm. The movement revealed the tattoo of the Wolf, the Moon, and the Sword, a twin to the one Shade still had on his left forearm.

Sometimes he thought he should scrape the thing off. One more identifying marker he didn't need, a symbol of a dead past...but he'd never do it. Nor would Instance. They fought together back when their country was more than ashes.

Never mind the thirteen tick marks around the tattoo. No one remembered what those meant, not these days.

"I was." Shade sat back in his chair, muscles aching.

With luck, the trappers were stuck on the north side of the Bridge tonight. Either they'd give up the chase or think him not stupid enough to cross continents in foul weather. *They're not wrong.*

Gambler though he was, Shade was no fool; he crossed the Bridge in daylight, hours ahead of those chasing him.

Instance perked up. "Was?"

Shade scrubbed a tired hand over his face before stopping himself and yanking it away. It made his scars itch. "I was pursued from Median two days ago," he said. "It seems some of our countrymen answered Olor's call for Night Rider trappers."

"They *what?*"

"They're calling themselves *venatores.*" Shade scowled.

"Fuckers." Instance pushed his food away. "I've lost my appetite."

"Tell others you see on the road," Shade continued, his voice clipped and short. "They're more skilled than the Olorians."

"I will." Instance's brow furrowed beneath his own hood. He was silent for a long moment, and Shade left him to think, idly listening to the *hospitia*'s background noise.

He heard a familiar female voice behind him but did not turn. That was Allesa, Gunstrum's daughter. Ever since he'd rescued her, Allesa thought herself in love with him, dreaming up stories about why they couldn't be together. Gunstrum tried to gently dissuade her, but like most parents, he failed.

Shade avoided her. Making connections that could be used against them was dangerous for a Night Rider...and she was almost two decades his junior.

"Shade! It's so good to see you." And now Allesa, gorgeous, buxom, and blonde, leaned over their table. "Can I get you anything?"

"Your house special, please." He met her gaze, ignored her smile.

"Anything else special tonight?" She batted her eyes.

"No, thank you."

"Are you sure, Shade? You know I'll always make time for you, if you know what I mean." Allesa reached out to touch his arm; Shade shifted away.

"Quite." He narrowed his eyes, wishing she'd get the hint.

"Well, if you change your mind, you know where to find me." One more smile, and she finally retreated, leaving the tension to slowly eek out of Shade's body.

Beneath his cloak, he eased his fingers off the dagger tucked into the right side of his belt. He'd barely noticed his hand finding it.

Instance watched her go with a smile. "Wish she'd look at me like that."

Shade snorted. "You're welcome to her."

"So long as I have your blessing." Instance laughed before sobering and lowering his voice. "Do you think they went for you first on purpose?"

Instance knew. He remembered.

"Perhaps." Shade shook away Allesa's presence. It wasn't her fault. She was young enough to think him glamorous, and he was old and worn enough to just want her gone. "I would say it was chance, but I no longer believe in coincidence."

"Do they *know*?" Instance's eyes went wide.

"Don't be ridiculous." Shade met his gaze and saw a bit of shame there, in with the fear. "If they knew, it would be Olorians hunting for my head, not Evendarians."

Instance choked out a laugh. "Or maybe you're just the easiest to recognize."

"Perhaps." Shade flashed his teeth in a sneer. It made him look cruel, with twin scars framing his right eye and mouth and running diagonally down his face. Shade knew he looked the part a killer. "Or they noticed the price on my head. It's hard for Evendarians to find a profit these days."

"Do they think that by stopping you, they'd stop the rest of us?" Instance frowned thoughtfully.

"I doubt it." Shade shook his head. "Except—" Suddenly, Instance sat up straight, and Shade's instincts lit on fire. "What is it?"

"Nine men just walked in," Instance replied, shifting his weight and loosening his sword in its scabbard. "They're all hooded, but not Night Riders. One's moving to the bar, speaking to Gunstrum."

A wave of cold trickled down Shade's spine. "Nine? You're certain?"

5

VENATORES

There were eight in a normal Olorian patrol. Nine men, however...nine men chased him here.

"Yeah. The one at the bar's removed his hood. He looks Evendarian." Instance's voice went tight.

Shade shifted slightly, gathering his feet under himself and resting his weight on the balls of his feet. He said nothing. He didn't need to.

"They're wearing schiavonas, too." Instance scowled.

The schiavona was the traditional sword of an Evendarian, with a blade heavy enough for chopping but light enough to wield in one hand. Centuries of Evendarian legionaries carried them in victorious battles, right up to the Fall, where they lost everything. Shade sighed.

He did not want to kill Evendarians. Not his countrymen, not when there were too few to protect Evendarians against the harsh hand of Olor. He chose to run rather than harm them, hoping the fools would find Night Riders too difficult prey and give up. *I swore to protect them once. Must I now kill them?*

A softer man might weep.

29

"Whatever he's asking, Gunstrum's shaking his head—but one of them's noticed us," Instance said. "He's pointing."

"Damn."

Shade loosened his schiavona in her scabbard, his left hand nudging the swept basket hilt while his right found a dagger, drawing it half out of the sheath. The Night Riders' eyes met, neither turning, even as approaching footsteps drew close. One advantage both had was that they were in an Evendarian *hospitia*. No *venator* would wish innocents harm, not even to earn a fat bounty.

At least he hoped not.

Counting footsteps, Shade took the last sip of his ale and watched Instance settle back in his seat. Both were seasoned fighters, had been since before the Empire fell. More importantly, they knew one another. They also knew that, for a pair of Night Riders, nine trappers were no threat, especially in a raging storm only a fool would venture into. A fool...or Night Riders who knew the weather would wash away their tracks. They only had to escape, not win a battle.

"Excuse me." The voice that came from behind Shade had an accent like his own, clipped and Imperial. Where had this *venator* come from that he'd fallen so far?

Instance answered in his country twang. "What do you want, boy?"

"My friends and I would like to speak to you outside." The courteous words were not a request.

"About?" Shade didn't turn; he watched the shadows on the wall behind Instance. Two were larger than the others; the speaker brought a friend, but the others hung back.

The *hospitia* had a porch, not a large one, but shelter all the same. Nine against two, in a crowded area; would the trappers disarm them and go for the capture, or would it be death? He really didn't want to kill Evendarians today.

"Does that matter?" The youthful voice was harder now. Impatient.

Shade let out a breath and then nodded to Instance. Both rose, keeping their hands well away from their weapons. No need to frighten the children yet. He met the leader's eyes. "I suppose it does not."

The leader wasn't as young as his voice sounded; he was at least thirty, old enough to remember a different and better Evendar. But he was well-fed, even a little overweight—uncommon, in a world where Evendarians were legally slaves. And yes, his clothes were finer, too. *This one makes a living pleasing Olorians.* Shade fought back a snarl, keeping his face blank. He still did not want to kill the arrogant traitor.

The other trappers were nicely garbed, too, and wearing swords. That was illegal unless an Evendarian had a special permit. This was not their first time working for Olorians, and anger swirled through Shade as he wondered what *other* tasks they might have done. Hunting escaped slaves? Bullying taxes out of poor Evendarians? Worse?

Under the watchful gaze of the *venatores*, the Night Riders exited the *hospitia*. Shade paused only to nod reassuringly at Gunstrum, who stood behind the bar, wringing a dishtowel this way and that in his hands. Common Evendarians saw Night Riders as heroes, as those who dared do what others only dreamt of—but not to Olorians. . . or their minions.

I will not hunt you, *my countrymen, but nor will I allow myself to be taken and turned over to Olorian torture.*

The doors slammed shut behind them, with three of the trappers behind the pair and six ahead.

The wind, already howling harder than when Shade arrived, picked up his cloak and tore it right, trying to plaster his hood into his face. Shade did not move, staring ahead, his mind racing behind blank eyes.

Ten horses stood outside Gunstrum's, still saddled and ready to ride. *They only expected one.* Their leader wanted to take no chances; braving the storm must seem safer than trying to keep a Night Rider pinned up for the night.

Not a bad plan.

Except for one thing. Now there were *two* Night Riders. What did the leader plan to do? Greed said to take them both, but could he hold two?

6

GREED AND VIOLENCE

S hutters slammed shut across the street; Weltil's people wanted nothing to do with this. They were survivors of the Second Great War and its aftermath; getting involved in Olorian "justice"—even that perpetrated by Evendarians—was fatal.

Even Gunstrum stayed inside. That wasn't disloyalty. He knew when to quit.

Gunstrum also knew that *someone* would die today. Maybe two someones.

Maybe nine.

"Disarm yourselves." The leader said. Shade could hear his chest puffing out, saw two others exchanging satisfied grins out of the corner of his eye.

Oh, they were proud, weren't they? They'd done the impossible and caught *two* Night Riders. Shade's lips twitched into a cool smile. *Don't count your victories until your enemies are dead, boy.*

"Who're you to demand a man give up his sword?" Instance cocked his head, smiling innocently. "Here I thought it was only Olorians who say it's illegal for an Evendarian to be armed with something more than a butter knife."

"You are guilty of violating various laws—"

"Olorian laws?" Shade kept his voice cold despite the fury boiling within him. "The same laws that name you *slave*?"

"I am no such thing," the leader hissed.

"They would have you as such." Shade finally turned his head to look at the pompous rat. "As they would have all of us." He did not mention the brand on the back of his neck, scratchy and uncomfortable under his ponytail. "Yet you kneel to the Olorian queen and do her bidding like a good slave, don't you?"

"I am more than you could ever hope to be! Surrender yourself!"

"No."

"We will kill you if we must. The price is less, but—"

An elbow to the face killed that sentence; the leader swallowed blood and spat out teeth, staggering back and temporarily out of range. Immediately, Shade's sword flashed into his hand, the leather-wrapped grip cool against his palm. The silver blade glowed, distant lighting playing off its edges as Shade cut straight through one of their would-be captors' swords and disarmed another.

At his back, Instance wheeled into motion, and they made quick work of the *venatores*, disabling and disarming where they could. Neither feared taking another's life, but these were their countrymen. A long time ago, both had sworn to protect men like this, and even Shade—despite how many Olorians he'd killed—shied away from killing Evendarians.

Three long heartbeats later, their opponents laid scattered around them, groaning and winded. Together, they bolted for the barn, finding their mounts and throwing open stall doors to swing saddles over broad backs. No sane Night Rider would leave a horse behind, at least not a good one. Horses were treasured—meaning the difference between life and death. A well-trained one was worth killing for.

Jerking awake, Vic snorted and snaked his head toward his owner as if to bite him, only drawing back at the last moment. But he didn't fight the saddle or the bit, shaking off sleep perking up. Without even leaving the stallion's stall, Shade shoved his left foot in the stirrup and swung aboard, ducking his head as he urged his mount from the stall.

"Instance!" Quickly, he slammed his sword home into the scabbard. Glancing down, Shade wrapped the split reins around his left hand, catching a clump of Vic's mane in with them. In wet weather and close combat, hands and leather would often slip, and for a Night Rider, that meant death.

"Ready!"

"Let's move!"

Instinct prickled. *Why do I feel that this is far from over?*

A touch of his heels sent Vic shooting forward like a bow-strung arrow, and he felt Instance's horse right on his heels. It took his eyes a moment to adjust to the dark and windy sky as they burst from the barn, but when they did—

Vic skidded to a stop, almost throwing his rider from the saddle and splashing mud all around. As arrows split the sky right where Shade's head would have been, whistling inches from his face. Instance was not so lucky, and Shade's right hand snapped out just in time to catch his fellow Night Rider before Instance could tumble from the saddle, an arrow embedded in his left shoulder.

Howling in pain, Instance swore and caught his balance, calling down curses on all *venatores,* their grandchildren, and their second cousins. Thunder rumbled, and almost on cue, the sky opened up with pouring rain, drenching everyone within seconds.

Spurring Vic forward, Shade grabbed Instance's mount's bridle to urge the other horse along. Rain was useful, but it limited their options. He turned south down the Via Indus.

Only then did he risk a glance over his shoulder.

A horde of riders galloped toward them from the south. There were at least two dozen of them, perhaps more—it was hard to tell in the driving rain, and their approach couldn't be heard over the howling gusts of wind.

"Fuck!" He could barely hear his own voice.

The violent wind worked in the Night Riders' favor; arrows would be blown off course and away from their backs. But with more *venatores* coming from the south and water to the east, they were left with only one option—north. North, and the Bridge.

West would take them to Fiskell Bay. But a quick glance at the ground told Shade that the Bridge would be partially flooded out by now and slow to ford...at best. He threw another look over his shoulder at their trappers, judging numbers and distance. Not liking the answer that his gut gave him, he calculated again, but the result was the same.

The *venatores* would catch them at the Bridge unless something was done to delay the pursuit. Experience told him that there were far too many to fight, especially with a wounded comrade by his side. Shade was willing to take on a dozen by himself, perhaps more if he could twist circumstances in his favor, but not this many, and not like this. Besides, he wasn't too proud to run from his own countrymen, particularly if it kept more of the idiots alive.

There were trees to the left—not many, but perhaps enough to skirt Bridger's Bay and then move south—

Bending low in the saddle, Shade urged Vic on. His horse responded with a spurt of speed, sprinting off the road and into the small forest, cutting away from the cow path and up a small hill.

Instance kept pace with him, despite his wound, even through the raging stream where Vic nearly lost his footing and drowned both horse and rider. Finally, they reached a thicket, where Shade reined his mount to a stop, wheeling the stallion so he could rearrange the branches their passage disarrayed.

Meanwhile, Instance reached up and, with a hiss of pain, broke the arrow's shaft off from where it stuck out his shoulder. He gritted his teeth, swore again, and ripped the arrowhead out. "It's not bad."

"Good." Shade wouldn't call his old friend a liar. Not right now.

Not with enemies on their heels.

Shade turned to watch the forest, listening to thunder rumble in the distance. Neither Vic nor Instance had the stamina for a long chase. Shade had been on the road for far too long, and Vic was tired. So was he, but it was harder to explain pushing through exhaustion to a horse.

No matter what Instance said, he was bleeding and needed healing. A mage sure as hell wasn't going to be found in the middle of a storm, either, and wet bandages wouldn't do much good. Instance could still fight and ride, but he wouldn't be at his best. Even the slightest wound could worsen and get infected if left alone too long. This far from a healer, an infection could kill as readily as an Olorian sword.

Or an Evendarian one.

7

SACRIFICES

Several minutes passed before Instance finally whispered, "They'll find us, you know."

"Probably." Shade scowled. He was too tired for this, his muscles too heavy and mind too slow.

"Probably, hell." Instance's laugh sounded wet. "Last I checked, I've been on the road nearly about as long as you, and we both know that this wood ain't big enough to hide us, even in this mother of a storm. And we both know that we're going to lose if we turn this chase into a chase. There're too damned many of them, and we're both too tired."

"Then we make a fight of it."

Shade might not want to kill Evendarians, but he liked the idea of dying even less.

Thunder cracked again; lightning split the sky. There were shapes in the distance, approaching steadily. He couldn't hear shouting—though the wind could be carrying it away—and they probably haven't been spotted yet. It was only a matter of time.

"I know you want to kill those kids even less than I do," Instance whispered.

"We all choose our fates." The words of an old oath tried to drift through his mind; Shade ignored them.

"Damn right." Instance sucked in a breath and nodded calmly. "You go; I'll distract them."

Shade twisted in the saddle to face him. "*What?*"

"I *said* for you to go." Instance turned to glare at him. "I'll lead them elsewhere. Given time, you can make it across the Bridge."

"They hunt *me*."

Instance shrugged with hardly a grimace of pain. "They hunt a Night Rider. One'll do as well as another. They're not going to give up until they get one of us, and that means one of us has to die here. *You* can't. Me, I'm expendable."

Bile rose in Shade's throat. "I mislike your tone." The words came out stilted. Formal. All wrong.

Instance grinned. "You're in good company. I bet they're going to mislike a bunch of things about me."

How could he ask a friend—*another friend,* pointed out the traitorous voice of his past—to sacrifice for him? How could he refuse when Instance offered? They both knew what was at stake. They both knew Shade would hate himself for this...yet he had not survived ten years of Olorian torture and slavery to die on the road, in the dark and rain, with no one to know *why*.

There had to be another way.

"And if you're captured?" His mind whirled through possibilities. *I have lost enough friends already in this goddamned war! Not this one. Not this time.*

"Your secret is safe." Instance smiled sadly. "I can hold out a day. We both know they'll give me to the Olorians. They'll have their sport and then kill me as publicly as they can. I'll die as a Night Rider."

Shade was too drained to weep, even for an old friend. He'd grown so cold over the years, too cold. Too detached. "There are always—"

"There isn't. We both know it. Stop arguing," Instance said. "I still remember the words, you know. *'And above all, this I swear to fight, and if need be to die, to—'"*

"Don't say it," Shade hissed.

Instance didn't. He just met Shade's eyes steadily, waiting.

Shade swallowed. Tried not to remember.

He knew those words. He'd sworn them, too.

"Let me do this last thing," Instance said. "For Evendar."

A lump rose in Shade's throat. "For Evendar," he repeated and then held out his right hand. "Ride well."

"Never forget." Instance nodded as their hands clasped, and they clung to each other for one moment, knowing it was the last time. With one last smile, Instance pulled away. He turned his horse without another word, breaking through the underbrush and riding toward the enemy.

Shade watched his back, pretending it was the rain blurring his vision. He could not afford to be crippled by grief, could not afford to remember the echo of another friend who said almost those same words, too many years ago—

Don't think about that now. Instead, he watched Instance vanish into the gloom, waited until he heard shouts that Instance was spotted. The other man would lead the *venatores* trappers on a merry chase. Perhaps he'd even get away. *Not likely.*

Swallowing, Shade turned, nudging Vic with his heels and heading northwest. *Forgive me, old friend.*

He was out of earshot before the sounds of metal ringing on metal filled the air, hunched low in the saddle to shield himself from the elements as best he could. The sick and empty feeling remained, making him burn to turn around, just to *try* to make a difference, to see if he might be in time to save Instance's life—or at least die beside him.

Were Shade a little less conscious of his duty...but he was not.

The ride to the Bridge wasn't long, despite the weather. Shade tried to keep his mind on the rising elements and not on his friend's sacrifice. Instance made his choice; a true friend would honor that.

The wind picked up still more as he rode. Shade barely dared canter Vic as the gale grew worse. Galloping was out of the question, for the safety of horse and rider both. His cloak was reasonably waterproof, but Shade was soaked to the bone by the time he reached the Bridge, barely to keep his hood up, even to shield his eyes from the driving rain.

The first miles weren't bad; the Bridge was wider at its base, and while there were few trees to block the wind, at least the land beneath Vic's hooves was solid and mainly dry. Shade slowed to his horse to a trot, a good, ground-eating pace that they could keep up for as many hours as needed. Crossing the entire Bridge in one night was impossible; what he needed to do was make it past the narrowest point, and then he could rest in relative safety on the other side.

The Bridge grew narrower as they continued and felt even more exposed in the dark, like a tiny split of gray-brown land peeking out of the water. Waves roared in from the east, crashing over what little remained of the southern breakwater and dragging rocks away with every ebb. As they continued, the very sand beneath Vic's hooves seemed to move, and the stallion shifted uneasily, snorting when Shade drew him to a halt.

Vic shivered. Shade sucked in a deep breath, ignoring the old burn in his chest. If he had any luck left, the rest of the water flowing across the Bridge would be shallow enough to pass. Angry waves splashed across the sand at random intervals and completely covered some of the land he could see, swirling dangerously and looking eager to carry the entire Bridge away. He could only see the first fifty feet in the darkness—fifty feet of a thirty-mile-long causeway, but Shade knew he had to risk it.

Patting Vic on the neck, he urged him into the ankle-deep surf. After less than a hundred yards, Vic balked. Added leg pressure only made the big stallion shake his head and back up. Shade sighed. Only a fool would ride the Bridge at night in the middle of a gale, and even then, the fool's horse hadn't been consulted. Especially when it was a tired and waterlogged horse.

"Come *on*." Shade squeezed his legs again, urging Vic forward. "We don't have time for this, and it will only grow worse as the night goes on."

Vic snorted and stamped a hoof, splashing water and then pawing for good measure. Further attempts only made the stallion toss his head, and when Shade kicked him, he backed up another step, kicking for good measure. Swearing at him didn't help, either, even in two different languages. Finally, Shade dismounted.

"Let's go." He pulled Vic forward by the reins. The stallion only looked at him dubiously out of wide brown eyes, whites showing. He swore under his breath. "This Bridge and I have a history, boy, but it hasn't killed me yet. Let's just get this over with."

He clucked his tongue and patted Vic again. Finally, step by step, the horse followed, first into the surf and then into knee-deep water as it washed over the bridge. Vic tossed his head, snorting, and picked up the pace; under other circumstances, the horse *liked* water, but his instincts told him that this was stupid and dangerous.

Shade grimaced. Vic was right. Being out here *was* stupid and dangerous, but there was no other way. Side by side, horse and rider trudged across the Bridge, taking mile after mile and moving through water that ranged from ankle-deep to Shade's waist—but at least there was solid ground underfoot.

They trudged forward together for what felt like a lifetime. Telling time was almost impossible in the dark. The moon was buried somewhere up there in the storm clouds, and the wind whipped at Shade's face every time he looked upwards to find it.

Glancing forwards during flashes of lighting didn't help, either; thick fog rolled in before they made it half past a mile onto the narrowest part of the causeway, obscuring his view of anything but the few yards in front of his face. So, he kept his head down and let his stallion bury his face against his shoulder. Together, they took one step after another, wet and cold but refusing to quit.

The storm slowed twice as if to mock them and then roared back to life stronger and more violent than ever before. However, the third calm held, the fog finally lifted.

Shade could now see the horizon ahead between distant lightning strikes, estimating they were about halfway across the eleven-mile-long midsection of the Bridge. He remembered this place, had spent a nightmare battle here once, one that changed his life and changed the world. *Don't think of that now.*

It was too easy to lose himself in the past during the storm. Gritting his teeth, Shade focused on the wind and rain, on how tight his chest was and how wet and cold his bones felt. Anything but the past.

Finally, after they trudged into wider ground, the weather calmed. As he and Vic walked, the hard rains turned into a gentle drizzle. Lighting still split the sky every few minutes, warning Shade that the gale was far from over. Perhaps he was in its eye, as the warmth in the winds hinted, but he would take any break he could get. Perhaps his luck would hold until he reached Coelera, at the head of the Bridge. *Then again, maybe not.*

He wanted to stop before Coelera and not only to rest Vic. Shade could use sleep, too. And maybe food. But at least he wasn't thirsty, not with how drenched he was.

As dawn approached, his ears picked up the sound of hoof beats. Multiple hoof beats.

Even as he whirled to face the distant noise, he knew what he would see. Sure enough, *venatores* bore down upon him again. There were fewer of them now—only six—which meant that Instance sold his life dearly. Or they'd taken him, and this was all that was left to chase him with *venatores* needed to guard their prisoner.

Again, and much to Shade's surprise, tears prickled in his eyes, but he shook off the sudden emotion. They'd finally made a mistake. He would make them pay for it.

He swung back into the saddle, loosening his sword in her scabbard.

45

Shade's creed was simple: *Save those you can. Avenge those you can't.*

He would not forget Instance's sacrifice. And someday, he would tell the world of it. But not today.

Bending low in the saddle, he swung Vic towards the enemy to avenge his friend.

8

—·—

RETRIBUTION

The six remaining *venatores* clearly did not expect Shade to turn back towards them. Their shouts carried to him on the half-dying wind, and they pointed at the Night Rider as he drew his sword and urged his mount on.

Vic, well-trained calvary mount that he was, lowered his shoulder and bounced off the lead *venator's* horse, throwing the rider off balance and making his mount shy left. Unbalanced, the *venator* forgot about swinging his sword and grabbed for the horse's mane—but by the time his hand made it there, a silver-bladed schiavona separated his head from his shoulders.

It bounced, and the sweet smell of blood mixed with the salt smell of two seas before being drowned out by the drizzle. The body collapsed, spooking the *venator's* already unhappy horse, who bolted and dragged the body a hundred yards before stopping.

Twisting in his saddle, Shade carried his sword's momentum forward into the next rider, stabbing him in the left shoulder. The poor bastard tried a cross-body thrust, but he was right-handed, and Shade was on his offside. The *venator* was foolish enough to go for a killing blow, which slowed him.

Shade was content with a quick stab and the scream that followed.

By then, Vic's momentum carried him free of the enemy. Leaning back, Shade whirled his mount around, and Vic rocketed forward before the four uninjured *venatores* realized what was happening. Quick pressure from Shade's legs sent Vic after the two on the left, and his sword snapped back up.

He caught the first one, a redhead wearing a torn red tunic—did Instance get a piece of him?—under the arm when the fool raised his sword for an overhead strike. The artery gushed blood, and he collapsed from the saddle as Shade moved on to his next opponent.

"Look out!" This one's Evendarian accent was pronounced as he tried to warn his companions. He even got his sword up in time, aiming for Vic's neck.

Decent tactics. Disable the horse and spill the rider. Shade approved, or would have if he'd meant to give this traitor half a chance to live.

Not so much.

A touch of his heels and Vic bolted forward, slamming broadside into the *venator's* squealing chestnut mare. Shade parried the attempted slash, carried it wide, and buried a dagger lefthanded into the *venator's* neck. He left it there.

Three down, three to go.

A quick glance showed him the first enemy he wounded was running away. *How brave.* Shade spared him no other mind, turning Vic with his legs before leaping out of the saddle. The two other *venatores* had their horses turned around and galloped towards him as a team, barely a horse's width apart, which was about the stupidest thing they could have done.

Two quick strides right, and Shade slipped between the two, his sword arcing up. One slice left, one slice right—he cut into one rider's thigh and the other's shin. Both howled in pain, the one to the right cursing a string of obscenities that focused on Shade's long-dead mother.

That one had too much anger and adrenaline coursing through his system to realize that his shin was cut to the bone. He kicked his horse with his working leg, bearing down on Shade.

"Fucking whoreson!"

Shade cocked his head, squared up, and stood his ground.

"I'll fucking kill you!" But the *venator* kicked his horse too hard with that one good heel when he forgot the other leg wouldn't work. The confused animal swerved.

Seeing his opening, Shade danced to the rider's offside, grabbed his arm, and hauled him out of the saddle. The Night Rider's sword came down in a flash of silver, and blood splashed up; Shade twisted his head aside to keep it from getting into his eyes.

By the time he dropped the body and looked up, the last *venator* was struggling to turn his horse and stem the flow of blood from his left thigh at the same time. But he still glared at Shade with murder in his eyes, still had a sword in his hand, and was still a threat.

Part of Shade wanted to let him live, but these same men had murdered—or captured—his friend. They swore allegiance to the Queen of Olor, abandoning their countrymen, and for what? Money? A little comfort? The assurance that they, too, would not be hunted or enslaved?

Only a fool thought Nydein OlorIlliet would treat Evendarians with dignity. Particularly after this many years.

He was too fucking tired to prolong this fight.

Whipping his arm back, Shade flung his schiavona with all his strength. He watched it arc through the air, flipping end-over-end once, twice, and then a third time before it slammed into the last *venator's* chest. Spooked, his horse reared, and he flopped out of the saddle, gurgling his last before he hit the ground.

Scowling, Shade trudged the fifteen feet to him to pull his sword free. He could still see the last *venator* in the distance, riding south for all he was worth.

He could follow. The other man's horse was likely as tired as his own, judging from how it weaved left and right. Vic was young, fit, and better bred. Shade *could* catch him.

Or he could let the Bridge eat him.

He sighed. "I hate this place."

How many bodies had been left on the Bridge in past years, how many swept out to sea? Was it the storm that made the air feel heavy, or the weight of too many souls left to wander when their bodies were left unburnt? Shade shook himself. Now was not the time to be maudlin.

Nor was this the time to think about battles past. He could not change wrongs already visited upon his people. He could only move forward. Fight while he could.

His muscles ached, and he burned for sleep, but thanks to these fools, he now had more work to do before he could rest.

9

— • —

PRAYERS

Rounding up the *venatores'* horses took the most time. Fortunately, most of them were tired, too, though three looked at Shade with big, white eyes, mistrusting this man who'd butchered their owners. He spent precious time calming them, hoping the storm wouldn't come back before he could get off the damned Bridge.

Loading the five dead bodies back onto their mounts took less time, even though he had to retrieve the one head he'd removed. He secured each to the saddle, tied the horses off in a line, and remounted Vic. The gray craned his neck to give Shade a disgruntled look but didn't otherwise object. He was tired, too.

Shade didn't want to know how long he'd been awake. It was day, now. A stormy day, but daylight all the same. That meant he'd gone over eighty hours, two full days, without sleep—unless one counted abortive naps snatched in the saddle, which he didn't. No wonder he felt drunk.

Vic's heavy footfalls as he trotted through the Bridge's last miles said the same. Finally, they neared the head of the Bridge, where trees started encroaching, and the causeway grew wide enough that Shade couldn't see either shore.

He reined Vic to a halt. "Far enough," he muttered.

Vic just dropped his head to nibble at the grass underfoot as Shade dismounted. Only long years of experience kept his knees from buckling; he leaned on the horse for a moment before pushing away.

There would be time for fatigue later. Pulling a collapsible multi-tool out of his saddlebag, Shade unfolded it to reveal a hatchet. The blade was short but sharp, well-oiled and part of a seventeen-piece multi-tool developed centuries earlier by the Evendarian army. Such things were hard to find these days; Shade spent a year trying to track one down before a fellow Night Rider gave one to him.

Multi-tool in hand, Shade stalked towards the tree line. With the small hatchet, he started hacking branches off trees, sawing the large ones and cutting the smaller ones right off. He could have used his schiavona—she was sharp enough—but it felt *wrong*, so he only resorted to that when he ran out of easy-to-acquire branches.

Finally, he assembled enough wood to build a pyre large enough for the five bodies. Most of the wood was wet, which meant it wouldn't burn well, but wood from deeper in the pocket of trees was drier, so Shade positioned that on top.

Returning to the grazing horses, he pulled each body off their backs, hauling them one by one to his makeshift pyre. Shade laid them side by side, careful to fold each *venator's* hands over their chest. He contemplated the placement of the one removed head for a long moment before deciding he had not the energy nor the desire to remove four other heads. Should he burn their heads at their feet like traitors? Perhaps.

Were they traitors? Not under Olorian law, for sure, but Shade cared not for Olorian law. In an Evendarian court, assuming one still existed, a savvy lawyer would've argued that their actions didn't properly constitute *knowing* treason...and Shade was tired of seeing his people turned against one another.

He hated this world. Hated what his nation had become, hated the Olorians who turned a once-proud people into animals fighting over scraps. Fifteen years ago, Evendarians would not have hunted Evendarians so openly, not at any price.

Now he had five of his countrymen to burn. Whether or not they deserved it, he would treat them with respect.

Returning to Vic, Shade pulled a firestarter out of his saddlebag. It was one of the few magic items he was willing to carry. Shade hated magic and didn't care who knew it—but magic was useful for some things. It sure as shit beat standing there for an hour trying to get wet wood to light on fire, particularly with his limbs leaden and still soaking wet.

Shade glanced at the sky. That, and another storm was coming.

The firestarter was a brown stone about the size of his hand, polished and smooth. Shade didn't know what kind of rock the thing was and didn't care; he knew enough about magic to know that magic was based in the earth, and mages needed stones to work magic. A potent enough mage could magic a stone to work for anyone.

Shade had as little ability to use magic as your average Evendarian—which was to say none. But he could tap his fingers on the stone in the required pattern, touching it against the wet wood of the pyre. Sparks flew, and within moments, the fire raged.

The bodies caught quicker than the wet wood, which smoked profusely, filling the air with a musty, earthy smell. Shade resisted the urge to step back from the pyre. Instead, he tugged his hood up to cover his head, kissing his knuckles and offering that obeisance to the Lady by casting his hand away from his face, palm facing upwards.

For a proper funeral, there would not be mud and blood caked under his nails, and his clothes would be clean...but he would do what he could.

Glancing at the fire one more time, Shade bowed his head and spoke in the old tongue.

"Verenda Legata, vel quodcunque nomine mavis, mater, domina, et aperitor viae, tuam gratiam voluntatemque rogo ut venatores domum ad te ducas. Dona ei tuam clementiam et tuum lumen. Suum finis principium sit et Suum legatum dignum suae vitae sit."

It was an old prayer, more complicated than the ones practiced today. But the words rolled off his lips as easily as they had in the days of his youth.

"Were you a priest?"

10

SURVIVORS

S hade whirled around at the sound of a new voice, his hand flying to his sword. He had the schiavona half-drawn before he recognized the sole surviving *venator* from the earlier fight; the man was still bleeding from his shoulder wound, pale and haggard.

The pungent smell of blood cut through the sharp scent of damp wood and flesh burning, mixing the three together in an unpleasant barbequed mess.

"You speak the old tongue." The words were a raw whisper. The boy—because this *venator* was barely more than a boy, maybe eighteen, probably not that old—stared at him with big brown eyes that begged Shade to make sense of the violence.

"I do. And I am not." Shade sheathed his sword. He was too tired to kill this boy. Too tired of the slaughter, too tired of watching his people die.

"But were you?"

Shade tried not to look at the boy. Blood loss made his skin as pale as an Olorian's, and his sunken eyes made him look even younger than he probably was. Wild brown curls framed a too-innocent face—this boy tried to kill him not an hour earlier. He would not pity him.

"That is not your business." Shade let his eyes flick to the boy's shoulder. "Put pressure on that if you don't want to bleed out."

"You're not going to kill me?"

He cocked his head. "Did you follow me hoping that I would?"

The boy gulped.

"Find your own fate. I will not deliver you to the Lady without just cause."

Turning away, Shade remounted Vic, whose steady presence kept the dead *venatores* horses from wandering off. He'd sell those horses later; leading them around would slow him down, and leaving them loose would only get Olorian attention.

"You're going to leave them burning?" The boy gestured at the pyre with his good arm.

"They're your friends. You should watch over them." Shade adjusted his cloak, settling into the saddle, and continued without looking up. "Say a prayer for them in a language you understand."

The boy stared. Gaped.

Finally, in a small voice, he whispered: "Let your future be of light. Let your end be a beginning. And may your legacy be worthy of your life."

Shade nudged Vic into motion just as a rustling came from the trees to his right. His head snapped around, catching a glimpse of yellow eyes staring at him.

No.

That was surely his imagination.

Shade was too tired to make it too many miles past the head of the Bridge, and Vic wasn't much better. The dead *venatores'* horses were even worse off, and if he didn't let them rest, they'd get him next to nothing. Shade wasn't particularly worried about his profit margin—making money off those he killed wasn't exactly new to him, but it felt *wrong* to profit off Evendarians.

Mostly.

They *had* tried to kill him.

He made in the thickest trees he could find, a mile northeast of the Via Pontis. There, Shade pulled the saddles off all six horses but left the bridles on the *venatores'* mounts. He tied them off to a line between two trees, loose enough that they could graze but not wander off. Vic, he allowed to roam.

Muscles screaming with fatigue and lightheaded from exhaustion, Shade peeled his still-wet clothes off and changed into his spare set, scowling. He'd hoped to save that clean set for after a bath, but the deluge he endured on the Bridge was anything but.

It was also *cold*, and his limbs wanted to shiver. Sickness couldn't be forced aside by sheer force of will, either, so Shade wrapped himself in his spare cloak, kept dry by his saddlebags, and then nestled into his other cloak. That one was well-oiled and dry on the inside. Good enough.

Sleep claimed him almost immediately, but not before he thought he glimpsed yellow eyes watching from the distance.

Two days later—well-rested, but no cleaner—Shade rode into Coelera. Once a significant trading port at the head of the Bridge, Coelera's heyday came and went several centuries earlier. Two sacks during the First Great War doomed the city to second-rate status, as did the expansion of Cirantium, another port further east in the Sea of Cirus.

But Coelera would do. Large enough to boast multiple *hospitia*, taverns, and bars of ill repute, the city had a thriving Evendarian black market and a tolerance for Olorians barely skin deep. No one dared *do* anything to make an Olorian's life difficult, of course—that earned you a quick trip into slavery or worse—but people flouted Olorian law more eagerly in Coelera than most towns.

It was a good place to be a Night Rider. Almost as good as Qelldoria, Evendar's famous haven of licentiousness and luxury, and not hundreds of miles south.

Shade found a horse trader at sunset, just as the market was growing feisty. Olorians went home at dark; their traditions said evenings were to be spent with family. Evendarians grew a little braver in the dark.

Not that Shade knew anything about that.

"Selling?" The horse trader was a one-eyed woman with gray hair and muscles to put a strongman to shame. She was two inches taller than Shade, too.

"These five." He gestured at the *venatores'* horses. "Not the gray. You can have the tack, too."

"Sure about that?" She squinted. "I'd pay you as much for the gray as the others combined."

"I am aware."

"Pity." The horse trader sighed. "I suppose they're decent. I can offer you a hundred twenty-five sestertii each. Six-twenty-five total."

Shade let his eyebrows rise. "You and I both know you can sell nags for that."

She grinned. "Yeah, but how long do you want to drag them around for? I also won't ask where you got them from." A shrug. "But I'll throw in another seventy-five sestertii for the tack. Call it seven hundred even."

Seven hundred sestertii was more than enough to keep Shade and Vic fed and on the road for months. Not that Shade was terribly worried about money; he took enough purses off dead Olorians that he never went wanting. He'd starved before, but never as a Night Rider.

"Done."

Detaching the reins of the lead horse from Vic's saddle, Shade washed his hands of the *venatores'* horses and led Vic towards the nearest inn for a less metaphorical washing. His practiced eye picked out the sign for two, Val's Barstead and Praccus' Pocket.

There were two Olorians outside Val's Barstead, drinking heavily. Neither looked interested in trouble—one looked away in a real hurry when Shade glanced at him—but Shade still headed for Praccus' Pocket. He knew of the place; it was considered safer than most for Night Riders.

Then again, so was Gunstrum's.

At least the Pocket had a barn, complete with grubby stable hands. These two were twin girls, each missing opposite front teeth. The one on the right smiled, showing more dimples than her sister.

"You gonna help with Lleu's Lords?" the lefthand girl asked as her sister whispered sweet nothings to Vic and rubbed his neck.

Ornery and tired or not, that was the way to Vic's heart; he followed her like a lost lamb. Shade barely had time to snag his saddlebags and spare cloak before the stallion vanished into the musty stable.

"The what?" Shade's mind was a tad slow, but he was certain he'd never heard of whoever those people were. The name sounded like they were trying to be impressive. And failing.

"Lleu's Lords." She chewed the stick leftover from a goat stick, or maybe a chicken stick; they made the latter up here in the north, which Shade found odd. Some people even put *beef* on a stick. Goat sticks were normal. Other meat wasn't meant to be eaten on wood. "They say they gonna protect us, but ain't nobody to protect us from 'cept them."

"Fascinating." Shade's face didn't twitch, though he flexed his free hand. "Lleu is an Evendarian name."

She shrugged. "So's he. 'S why he's got one."

"Thank you."

He did not smile. One, because Shade was unfailingly polite but rarely friendly. He didn't *like* people, which was no excuse for rudeness but did not earn them smiles.

But the second reason was more important. With trouble in the air at the Pocket, no way was he getting a bath tonight.

Faex.

11

PROTECTION

T he interior of Praccus' Pocket was like that of a thousand other inns. The walls were stucco, painted off white to hide handprints but still give the place an old Evendarian-style look. The windows lacked glass—not a surprise—and the shudders were open now that the storm had passed.

The patrons were mostly Evendarian, with a few half-Olorians mixed in. Those were isolated off to one side, not quite shunned but not really in the thick of things, either. Everyone else sat together in clumps, laughter and conversations echoing around them. The Night Riders' customary table in the back corner was empty, too. A good sign.

Shade headed there without a word to anyone, settling in with his back to the wall, his hood still up, and his sword at his hip. No way would he disarm himself. Not with trouble in the air.

"You better pay for that, darling!" The barkeep grinned as a regular snagged a bottle from behind the bar, wagging her finger at him.

He laughed. "Put it on my tab, Nessie."

"Tab? You mean the one your wife told me she's not paying no more?" Nessie snatched the bottle back before he could drink. "Coin first. Drink after."

"Greedy grubber." Scowling, he slapped a copper aus on the bar, which disappeared down Nessie's cleavage.

She stuck her tongue out. "Greedy and with a business to run. I know you don't have much imagination, Bradus, but even you can conjure that."

Shade ignored the rest of their byplay, his eyes tracking right as someone whooped from the front of the room. *Dice players*, his mind reported, and he paid them no more mind.

At first glance, it could almost be an inn from before the Fall—from before the Olorians came to claim Evendarian lives and prosperity. But the cracks showed. One man to the left sported whip marks on his face. Another hid a half-burned-off brand on the back of his neck with long hair. And almost everyone glanced towards the door periodically, just in case an Olorian showed up.

Despite his experience a few nights ago, Shade was probably the least worried about that.

"You're a Night Rider." The waiter, approaching to take his order, stopped cold. "You here to help with Lleu's Lords?"

Shade cocked his head, watching the waiter from under the shadow of his hood. Like the twins outside, he was still a boy, probably fourteen. The freckles on his face stood out in stark contrast to his nearly bald head, where bruises decorated his skull in purple and black.

Old enough that the Olorians consider him a man and would hurt him as such, Shade thought but did not say.

"For now, I will settle for wine. Red, if you have it."

"It's expensive."

"Bring me your best bottle. And one glass." Shade slid two bronze sestertii across the worn table.

The boy's eyes widened. "On it."

He was off in a flash, grinning. What he said to Nessie—who looked enough like him to be his mother, or maybe sister—Shade ignored. If he couldn't have a bath, he was damned well going to have good wine.

Or at least what passed for good wine in this place. It was better in Val's Barstead, but there were Olorians there. Shade wasn't in the mood to pick a fight tonight.

His wine showed up quickly, brought by the grinning boy, who bounced as he caught the copper aus Shade tossed him. Shade didn't watch him go, instead pulling the cork and sniffing at the wine.

Not vinegar. A good start.

Then Shade read the label and scowled. It was a New Gloria River Red—a decent vintage with an unfortunate name. *3001.* An even more unfortunate year, marked by the start of the Second Great War and the beginning of a betrayal.

Still, it wasn't the wine's fault Shade was a morose bastard. He poured a glass, sipped it, and sat back to let his muscles burn out their tension. Listening to the hum of Evendarian voices was relaxing, was a reminder that *this* was what he fought for—not for vicious *venatores* who sought to profit off their own countrymen.

The boy approached again; Shade ordered the house special without looking at the menu. After enough days on the road eating jerky and stale bread, he wasn't picky. It arrived quickly, and Shade ate absently, thinking that maybe he *could* take a bath. It wouldn't be warm, not here, but a decent scrub would—

"Time to pay up, Nessie."

Shade looked up from his food to study the newcomer. He was heavyset and had bulky muscles gained from lugging heavy loads. A carter, maybe? His dancing blue eyes and fierce smile said he knew he was the most dangerous man in the room, and his swagger proved it.

Nessie crossed her arms. "I should tell you to piss up a rope, Lleu. Particularly after what happened to Kell."

"Ain't my fault an Olorian took him."

"*Tried* to. You heard what they did." She leaned across the bar, and for a moment, Shade thought Nessie might slap Lleu, but she didn't.

"They did what Olorians do. Can't be helped." Lleu shrugged. "I'm sorry for your loss, but your husband and I have a deal."

"It *can't be helped?*" Nessie hissed. "Those Olorian bastards wanted Kell as a slave, and when he tried to fight, you—our 'brave protector'—were nowhere to be found. Instead, they laughed, raped him, and killed him in the street. Can't be helped? I shit on your prick."

Lleu threw his head back and laughed. "I like your spirit, Nessie. That's why I ain't gonna take that personally. Unless you don't pay up."

"I'm not paying you *faex*."

Faex was the most commonly remembered swearword from the old tongue; people liked it because it sounded like fuck and meant shit, which meant you got a two-for-one special on profanity.

Lleu lost his smile. "You want to keep this inn running, and you're gonna."

Nessie snorted. "You don't know squat about running this place, and you are as useful as an Olorian in the Lady's temple. Get lost."

"Get your husband, woman. This is between me an' him."

"My husband'll tell you the same thing."

"Praccus!" Lleu threw his head back and bellowed the name. "Get down here before your wife gets herself killed!"

"More likely, I'd knife your ass," Nessie muttered, fingering a blade.

"Praccus!"

"There's no need to shout." Praccus was a small man, a head shorter than Nessie, soft-spoken, and dark of hair and eye. "I'm right here."

He came down the stairs with a stack of blankets in hand, looking at Lleu like people shouted about death in his inn every day.

Then again, maybe they did. Evendar wasn't what she used to be.

"Then talk some sense into your woman before I kill her dead." Lleu drew a nasty-looking knife, a cross between a cleaver and a dagger.

Nessie scoffed and made a show of drinking some ale. Shade followed suit and sipped his wine; that knife was good for threatening but was too big and slow to be efficient at much else.

Clearly, Nessie knew her shit.

"You never said anything about killing anyone," Praccus said, his voice still soft.

"Yeah, well, she's getting on my nerves."

Four men crowded up behind Lleu. One of them, a burly redhead, spoke up: "And we don't like *waiting*, Praccus. You know that. Someone's gonna get hurt if you don't pay up."

The others murmured agreement.

Shade sighed and put his wine down.

"I am wondering about the wisdom of our deal," Praccus said. "If you can't protect me from the Olorians, why am I paying you?"

The redhead laughed. "You're paying for protection from us, cunt licker."

"You say that like it's an insult." Nessie rolled her eyes. "But no woman's gonna let you near her duckies, so I think it might be envy, Cavus."

Lleu slammed his dagger down on the bar. "Enough of this shit. Pay up, or we start with Nessie."

Shade rose. "I think not."

12

CHOICES AND CHANCES

Lleu swung around, his dark eyes blazing. "Who the fuck are you?"

"Someone who will not stand for you abusing your fellow Evendarians." Shade moved forward, weaving through the tables and drawing his hood back as he walked.

A hush fell; most of the patrons turned to stare. Wide eyes found the schiavona at his hip—against Olorian law to wear—and traveled upward to the set of parallel scars cutting diagonally across his face from right temple to the left side of his jaw.

Lleu's four bullyboys crowded up behind him. One, with a crooked nose, cracked his knuckles, grinning. Another fingered a cleaver, much like Lleu's own.

"This ain't no business of yours, outsider," Lleu said. "You don't want no trouble."

"That's an interesting assumption for you to make, given the present circumstances." Shade cocked his head but never broke stride.

Two more steps took him to within arm's reach of Lleu, who realized too late that Shade wasn't stopping. His cleaver started to come up, but Shade caught Lleu's wrist in an iron grip, bringing his right knee up to smash into Lleu's knuckles. Yelping, Lleu dropped the cleaver.

His friends surged forward, but Shade ignored them. Instead, he clamped his left hand down on the back of Lleu's neck, propelling him forward and smashing his forehead off the bar. The blow wasn't quite enough to knock him out, but Lleu fell, sputtering and moaning, while Shade turned back to face the others.

That same left hand swept back to shove his cloak aside, revealing the silver hilt of his schiavona. Shade didn't draw, but his left hand, resting on the scabbard, did thumb the blade up an inch or two just to loosen her.

He met the redhead bully's—Cavus, Nessie called him—eyes while Lleu mumbled something insensible.

"My name is Shade."

"You're..." Cavus trailed off, jaw dropping.

"Yes." Shade took a step forward, cocking his head. "I am."

Cavus dropped his cleaver, backing up a step. One of the others went with him. The other two, including the crooked-nosed knuckle-cracker, glanced at Cavus in confusion but didn't move.

"It's still four against one," Crooked Nose said.

"I don't make a practice of killing Evendarians," Shade said. He still hated that the *venatores* forced him to, and he didn't want to hurt these fools—only to scare them. "And nor should you."

"We're just tryin' to scare them a little." Cavus' voice was tiny for such a large man. He skittered back another step.

"And you should not abuse your fellow Evendarians, either. The Olorians do that quite often enough, don't you think?" Shade's voice went sharp, and with it, his old accent; he pulled his fury back with an effort, softening his tone. "We are all less than nothing to them. Are you going to fight like animals for their amusement, butcher each other because they showed you that you should?"

"It's not your business," Crooked Nose said.

"Shut up," Cavus hissed.

Crooked Nose scowled. "We can take him."

"He's a fucking *Night Rider*, Diamus. Who the fuck wants to fuck with a Night Rider?"

Diamus of the Crooked Nose turned to stare at Shade. "You're a Night Rider?"

"Did I not say that? I thought the name would give it away."

"Shit." Diamus dropped his knife, which bounced off the floor and hit his friend in the leg. Luckily, it only scraped against his boots, but he still yelped.

Turning back to Lleu, Shade hauled him to his feet by the back of his tunic. Lleu was still glassy-eyed and useless, so Shade pitched him into the waiting arms of his friends. Lleu groaned as they caught him.

"I recommend you reconsider your line of work, gentlemen," he said. "And if you think for one moment that you can resume your little 'protection' racket when I'm gone, keep in mind that I am not the only Night Rider. I will make sure the others know to watch you."

Cavus gulped noisily.

Shade smiled. "And let's say that you don't want to find out what happens if I have to come back and deal with you again."

Lleu and his so-called lords fled, with the would-be bullies half-carrying, half-dragging their boss. Without another word, Shade returned to his table, sat down, and sipped his wine.

A few minutes later, Nessie approached.

"Thank you. You didn't have to do that." She swallowed. "Then again, I don't suppose any of you lot have to do what you do."

"Someone has to." *And I swore an oath.*

Thinking like that made a knot twist in his stomach. Instance swore an oath, too, one he fulfilled with far too much grace.

"Your meals and room will be on the inn tonight. Don't you think of payin', not after helping us like that," Nessie said.

"I appreciate the gesture, but I pay for services rendered. And I'm sure you can put the money to good use." Shade let his eyes flick to the rafters to his left, where a shoddy repair held them together.

Nessie crossed her arms. "Takes a brave man to argue with me, but I guess you've proven that."

"I have my moments."

"Is there anything else I can get you?"

He almost asked for a warm bath, but there was no telling if Lleu's idiots' gain in brainpower was temporary. If it wasn't, they'd likely come back tonight and try to kill him, and Shade preferred not to be caught naked in the bath. Fighting like that was just undignified.

"No need."

13

PROSPECT

The beds at Praccus' Pocket were as lumpy as Lucky always claimed. Climbing out of bed left Shade a hair less stiff than he was getting in, however, and at least he was no longer cold and wet. He still wanted a damned bath but contented himself with scrubbing himself using the washbasin. It was better than nothing.

Always an early riser, Shade was at the corner table downstairs before the dining room started filling with patrons. Nessie brought him so bread and honey in exchange for two *aus* and then delivered a steaming cup of dulce.

Dulce was a sweet, hot mint drink that Shade generally eschewed in favor of alcohol; however, today, he needed the warmth in his chest.

"You look a mite pale." Nessie frowned. "Couple healers here ain't bad, though they're expensive. Want me to have one of the girls grab you one?"

"No, thank you."

"You sure?" She crossed her arms. "If money's the issue, you did us a service, and Rander owes us a favor..."

"It is not, and I am sure. Thank you." Shade would not tell her that magic healing didn't work on him.

71

Revealing that weakness was stupider than he was, even at his sickest. Besides, he could suffer through a chest cold and survive. Healable or not, he was hard to kill.

"Have it your way." Shrugging, Nessie headed back to the bar and left Shade with his dulce and bread. At least both were warm.

He was contemplating paying for another night and crawling back into bed when a young man stumbled into his table.

"Hi."

Shade sipped his dulce slowly and said nothing, studying the young man. His new companion fidgeted when Shade remained silent, revealing good teeth and freckles. Maybe he was twenty years old, perhaps a little younger, with dark hair, blue eyes, and a slight droop to the left side of his face.

He was tall, too, tall enough that Shade would have to crane his neck if the kid wasn't bending over the opposite chair.

"You're Shade, right? The Night Rider?" the kid grinned again and then faltered when Shade didn't smile back. "I was looking for you."

"That much is obvious."

"I think you can help me. Or at least I hope you can." Another smile. "Maybe?"

Shade checked a sigh. "First, you have to tell me what you want help with."

"Oh. Right. Sorry." He blushed. "I want to be a Night Rider."

Oh, Lady. Shade was afraid of that. Swallowing the last sip of his dulce, he sat back in this chair, ignored his creaking back, and eyed the kid. Maybe it would scare him off.

Unfortunately, it only made the nervous smile grow. "Can I sit down?"

"Do you think that's wise?"

"Um. I mean, you have to learn from a Night Rider to become one, right?" He gulped. "And you're a Night Rider."

"I am."

"Can you teach me? I learn quick."

"Not quick enough," Shade muttered before he could stop himself. "Sit down and tell me your name."

Glowing, the kid plopped into the chair. "Seril Rufio. I'm from here in Coelera. My parents both work in the port, but I want to make a difference. I want to *help*. I want to save people. Like you do."

"You'll start by never answering that question again, boy." *Seril Rufio, Coelera.* Shade committed it to memory. He would write it down later, in the code he kept his records in.

"But you just asked—"

"And a Night Rider's first line of defense is anonymity," Shade cut him off. "The *only* thing that protects your friends and family from your actions is that the Olorians don't know who you are. You take a name, and you *live* by that name. You never put it down, not even for a moment. And you don't come home."

Seril blanched. "I thought...I thought I could help here."

"And get those parents of yours killed?" Shade shook his head. "Do you know what happens to Night Riders when they're caught?"

Now was not the time to think of Instance.

Shade *prayed* he'd died in battle.

"I've heard things. Terrible things," Seril whispered.

"They're all correct. Any Night Rider who is caught alive is tortured to death. Publicly."

"Oh."

"That is what you risk. Every moment. Every day." Shade folded his hands. "That's what being a Night Rider is. One out of every three of us is caught."

"And dies?"

"Painfully."

Seril looked down at the tabletop, breathing hard. "Is it worth it? Do you help people?"

"Yes, we help people. We help those no one else will." Shade didn't count the number he'd saved. He didn't count the number he'd failed to save, either. But he counted the Night Rider losses. Every one of them. "Only you know if the risk is worth it."

Shade knew the answer before Seril spoke. Seril Rufio was one more in a long line of good kids—good *men* and good women—who were willing to follow him into this insanity. Evendarians to their core, they weren't willing to admit defeat any more than he was.

Twelve years after the Fall of Evendar, after the catastrophic end to the war where they lost their freedom, their hope, and so many lives, there were still Evendarians willing to fight. *Even with some of our own people hunting us.* Shade's heart clenched.

"I can do it. I know I can," Seril said.

"Then choose yourself a name, and I will find you a mentor."

14

MENTORS

He sent the kid home to gather supplies and say a last farewell to his family. Were he a little less tired, Shade would've insisted on leaving immediately, but the hacking cough that crept up on him that afternoon told him he needed another day of rest.

Much as he hated to admit it, Shade wasn't as young as he used to be. Time and hard use hadn't been kind to his body, either, so he would take rest where he could get it.

Seril returned to the Pocket right on time, meeting Shade outside the barn, bright-eyed and eager. By then, Shade felt marginally better; he wasn't cold all the time, and he'd killed the cough with whisky. The liquor helped him sleep, too. Never a minor consideration.

"I'm ready." Seril was more serious today, hopefully after a sober conversation with his dock working parents.

"Then come with me. Can you ride?"

"Yeah." Seril shrugged. "I won't fall off."

"Then we work on that first." Shade eyed the aged chestnut mare Seril held. There was gray around her muzzle, but she pinned her ears when he studied her too closely. *At least she has spirit.*

Seril deflated. "Not swords?"

Shade cocked an eyebrow. "Do you have one hiding in your bedroll?"

"No. They're illegal." Seril kicked at the dirt. "Figured you'd know how to get one. And teach me."

"Your mentor will teach you," Shade replied. "But first, horsemanship. Your ability 'not to fall off' may save your life someday."

"Why won't you be my mentor? I was meaning to ask."

Shade mounted Vic before answering. "I don't take students."

"Why not?" Seril clambered onto his own mare with little grace. Shade watched without comment, making a mental list of everything the boy had to learn.

"Because I'd get them killed."

They rode four blocks before Seril spotted two youngish women herding chickens. Shade could smell their shit from across the road, and listening to the birds squawk in offended protest set his teeth on edge. Most people walked around them without even noticing; this was clearly a daily occurrence on Coelera's gray and dirty streets, with the girls shouting good-natured insults at any Evendarian who got in their way.

"They're slaves," Seril said quietly.

Shade let his eyes slide over the pair. Both were on the thin side but not skeletal. Their frowning faces were creased and worn beyond their age, yet neither was bruised nor bloodied.

Both were clothed decently, too, which wasn't always the case for slaves. And they spoke to other Evendarians without hesitation or averting their eyes. Unhappy? Certainly. Beaten? Probably not.

"They are."

Seril looked at the women, at Shade, and then at the women again. "Aren't—aren't you going to help them?"

Shade shook his head. "You can't save everyone. You have to choose your battles...and choose them wisely."

"But you *can* help them. Right?"

"I could free them, yes. But then what?" Shade twisted in his saddle to look at the boy, whose blue eyes were big as dinner plates. Why did they have to be blue? They reminded Shade of family lost.

Don't think about that now.

He shook himself. "To free them, I'd have to steal them or kill their 'masters.' Either way, they can't stay in Coelera, so then I must take them away—but to where? Will they want to leave whatever family they have? And how will they support themselves?"

Seril's mouth opened...and then closed.

"You save those you can," Shade said more gently. "Night Riders must make the hard choices. It's not all glamorous fights and grateful people. Frequently, it's doing what you can, where you can, and living with the times you cannot."

Seril swallowed. "I think I understand."

"You don't yet. But you will."

They rode onwards, continuing past a small market where a group of Olorians were busy bullying an Evendarian fish merchant into better

77

prices. Shade *might've* intervened there, under just the right circumstances, but the Evendarian stood his ground well enough, and the Olorians took a halfway decent deal. Not the merchant's asking price, but not robbery.

Then again, the abrupt end to their negotiations might have come when they spotted Shade, saw his sword, and added two and two to get *Night Rider*.

One street from the edge of Coelera proper—the town's ragged, six-hundred-year-old walls stood almost a mile inside its modern boundaries—a voice rang out—

"Who the *blazes* do you think you are, Evendarian?" She spat the last word like a curse.

Shade twisted lazily in the saddle to face a raven-haired woman in the leathers of an Olorian courier. Based on the colors she wore, he guessed she was from Clas Gollep, the clan second in power only to Clas Illiet, Queen Nydein's own clan. Her haughty expression said she knew her worth, too—particularly compared to a mere Evendarian.

"If you must know, my name is Shade."

"You're wearing a *sword*." Glaring, she fingered her own blade, a falcata in the typical Olorian style. Its hilt was jeweled; no doubt she was *vas*Gollep, from the nobility.

He let his eyebrows float upwards in exaggerated surprise. "Am I? I didn't notice."

"Get off your horse. You're under arrest."

"I didn't know couriers had arrest authority these days," Shade replied. To his left, thankfully away from the courier, Seril squeaked.

Was that amusement or terror? Probably both.

"Anyone has the authority to put an uppity Evendarian in their place." Her upper lip curled into a sneer. "Now, get off that horse before I decide to take your companion as well."

Shade smiled. "You must be new at this."

Her jaw dropped. *"What?"*

Shade slid out of the saddle, drawing his schiavona and throwing his cloak over Vic's back in one fluid motion. "I am a Night Rider. I do not surrender to anyone."

If you squinted at his blade just right, you could make out the faintest outline of letters. But Shade did not give her the chance. The courier's sword was barely clear of its scabbard when he attacked.

It was not a fair fight, but Shade was rarely interested in fighting fair. He hadn't been in years. The courier had some skill—enough to intimidate Olorian yokels or helpless Evendarians—but she was slow. Terminally slow.

She barely blocked Shade's first attack, and her riposte was clumsy enough that Shade almost accidentally overpowered his parry. Back on balance, he twisted around her attempted counterattack, brought his sword slashing down to slice her arm open, and then stabbed her in the heart.

The courier fell in a heap.

Seril squeaked again.

Three Olorians—merchants or some sort of travelers, by the look of them—started forward, only to stop when Shade arched an eyebrow. He looked down at the body and then back up at them again.

"Either you can bury her, or I will," he said. "Your choice."

15

VERACITY

The Olorians chose to bury the courier, freeing Shade and Seril up to leave Coelera. Once out of the town, Shade set a quick pace, as fast as he thought Seril could stay on horseback for. The kid definitely wasn't up to a shouting conversation while clinging to his horse.

But Seril's old chestnut couldn't keep up that pace forever, so Shade took pity on the mare and slowed after a while.

"You'd bury someone?" Seril asked after he caught his breath.

The mare was still blowing. At least the boy seemed in decent shape. He wasn't too confident *on* the horse, but he wasn't a physical wreck.

He'd need a new horse, though, if he was going to survive.

"You know that's what the religion of Olorvas requires, do you not?" Shade asked. Seril was young enough that he'd grown in up an Evendar occupied by Olor. His parents may have raised him—secretly—in the light of the Lady, but Olorian religion was impossible to ignore these days.

Or escape.

"Yes, but it's *wrong*." Seril swallowed like he wanted to vomit. "To leave someone unburnt and rotting is to let them wander, lost and alone, for eternity."

Unbidden, an image rose in Shade's mind, of an unburnt body on an unlit bier—*Don't think of that now*. He pushed it aside as hard as he could, forcing himself to focus on the here and now, not the pain rising like acid in his throat.

"It's never wrong to respect someone else's beliefs. Doing so is what separates us from the Olorians. *They'd* bury us, despite what we believe. We will be better than that."

"Is that...what Night Riders do?"

"Yes. We also find buried Evendarians, where we can, and burn them."

"Oh." Seril looked down at his white-knuckled hands, which clutched the reins just a little too hard. "I just thought it was about fighting Olorians."

"We fight when and where we can. But we also help those who need it, when they need it. A Night Rider is never too proud to help *however* they're needed," Shade replied, "But worry you not. There is plenty of fighting."

Seril's smile was a fragile and nervous thing, the wide-eyed expression of a boy who'd never left home. "I want to be Warrior. I'll fight however I can."

"Warrior it is."

A day's ride brought them to Median, the very town Shade left those former slaves in less than a week earlier. Had it only been nine days? It felt like a lifetime. Coming here was risky; the other *venatores* were still out there, and they might circle back. But Shade judged that unlikely.

Besides, Median was the closest town to Coelera, and Seril—now Warrior—was not ready to weather a night on the road. And Shade still wanted that bath.

The Blue Horse usually had hot water, and Rhona Mus was one of the *hospitia* owners who Night Riders could trust more than most. Maybe with Warrior to watch his back, he'd finally get clean.

Shade glanced at the boy while they dismounted, watched his knees try to buckle, and watched him try to hide a yawn.

Or not.

Flipping a coin to the stableboy, Shade handed Vic over, grabbed his saddlebags, and gestured for Warrior to follow him. The boy trailed him on wobbly legs, clutching his cloak around himself like it was freezing out.

The Blue Horse was a larger-than-usual *hospitia*, comprised of three long, one-story buildings arranged in a horseshoe. The center courtyard lay behind a low wall and housed the bar, tables, and general revelry. In a time where Olorians claimed most successful businesses years ago, it remained Evendarian owned—mostly because Rhona straight-up paid tribute to Median's Olorian overlords.

Median was a more corrupt town than most these days. The Olorians in charge were more interested in money than hard work, which left room for Evendarians to keep their property...at a price. It wasn't kind, but it led to fewer physical abuses than you saw in many towns, so Night Riders generally didn't interfere.

"The usual table, gentlemen?" One of Rhona's waiters darted forward to greet them. He was a tiny man, with sparkling green eyes and carefully coifed hair, wearing an expression that said he was also there to cater to certain Olorian tastes.

Bile rose in his throat; Shade pushed it down. He could not save people from their own choices.

"Yes," he replied, watching Seril—Warrior—look around with wide eyes.

The Blue Horse's courtyard area was three times the size of the dining room at the Pocket. It was segregated, too; Rhona kept the Olorians to the front right, by the entertainment, and the Evendarians to the left. A fountain separated the two areas, bubbling with surprising energy.

Shade wondered who she bribed to keep that thing working.

"There's already someone there," the waiter said. "A friend of yours?"

"One can hope."

"Another Night Rider?" Damn, it was hard to think of the kid as Warrior when he wiggled with excitement.

Shade shot him a glare; the boy's eyes went wide. "If not, we have a problem."

"Right. The Pocket always leaves a table open. They do that here, too?" At least he wasn't stupid.

"They do."

As they weaved through the tables at the waiter's back, Shade let his eyes sweep over the crowd. The Olorians were raucous, cheering on the dancers—who, Shade noted, were behind a low barrier, probably to keep anyone from getting too handsy. Not that it would stop a determined Olorian, but Rhona had to try.

The Evendarians were quieter, mainly keeping to themselves. Some played at dice. But most ignored the cheering Olorians.

Much the same as in Median, then. Good.

The waiter dodged around a big man carrying dishes, allowing Shade a straight line of sight to the Night Riders' normal table. There was a cloaked figure seated there, but his hood wasn't up. Sharp blue eyes watched everything, framed by wrinkles in a hawklike face. His hair was steel gray, trending towards white, but he had the look of someone who could tear you to pieces, no matter what his age.

"Veracity," Shade said, stopping at the table with Warrior on his heels.

"Shade." The other Night Rider grinned. "You might be the only one who bothers to call me that nowadays. Everyone else gave up."

"You might be the only one who ignores the damned rules."

Veracity—Nelemart Ash, a former senior centurion in the Evendarian Army, of Ash's Army fame and one of the most wanted men in Evendar—shrugged. "It's not like they don't already hate me. It makes me warm and fuzzy inside every time I think about Nydein's reaction to me not being dead."

16

POTENTIAL

"It makes me warm and fuzzy inside every time I think about Nydein's reaction to me not being dead," Ash said.

Warrior's eyes darted between the pair. "I thought we weren't supposed to share our names with anyone?" He looked at Ash. "Or do you have two Night Rider names? Can we do that?"

Ash threw his head back and laughed. "When you're as old as I am, you can afford to ignore a rule or two. Even his. Call me Ash."

"I'm confused."

"So'm I." Ash's eyes slid to Shade. "I thought you didn't take students these days. Not unless you wanted them dead."

Warrior fidgeted. "That's not—I mean, I'm not—he said—"

"Sit." Shade slid into the chair across from Ash. "I was rather hoping you'd take him off my hands."

Ash chuckled. "I thought as much, but no can do. My own special idiot is off seeing to nature. Should be back in a few."

"You have a student?" Warrior perked up.

"Not quite as squeaky new as you." Ash chuckled and then met Shade's eyes. "I'll tell you about her later."

"Why not now?" Warrior blinked. "Oh. I don't need to know, do I?"

"Well, you're not stupid," Ash said. "You might survive a bit."

"A *bit*?"

"Enough, Warrior. He's playing with you." Shade sat back in his seat and listened to the music. It was an Olorian composition, of course—Rhona was far from stupid—but not half bad. There seemed to be some Evendarian influences, which meant this was probably composed after the Fall.

The same waiter approached and took their drink orders. Warrior ordered ale with wide eyes that said he wasn't used to being in a *hospitia* without his parents. Ash ordered a brandy for himself and ale for his unnamed student. Shade ordered a bottle of wine and one glass, avoiding Ash's knowing gaze.

Warrior looked like he wanted to ask when the bottle arrived, but Ash spoke up instead.

"Vicious should be back in a few. She's a good girl, despite the name she picked. Got a decent head on her."

"A girl?" Warrior's jaw dropped. "You let *girls* be Night Riders?"

"Let?" an unfamiliar voice asked. "Just try and stop me."

Warrior went beet red. "I didn't mean it that way. I just didn't—didn't—"

"Didn't think?" Vicious grinned. "Don't worry. Most people don't. Particularly the Olorians who end up with my sword up their gut."

Ash chortled. "Damn right."

Vicious plopped into a chair with no grace, swinging a leg over the back and almost kicking Warrior in the face. She shrugged when he glared.

She was a tall young woman of about twenty, with dark hair, darker eyes, and skin to match. Her smile was amicable, and she'd clearly been with Ash long enough to be riding the same mental horse.

Warrior looked at Vicious, wide-eyed. "You've killed people already?"

"Course I have. I've been with Ash for a couple months." She grinned.

"When do I get to help?" Warrior turned those dish-sized eyes on Shade, who snorted.

"When you've ridden with a Night Rider for more than ten minutes." He turned to Ash. "Who else is in the area?"

Ash sat back in his chair, thinking. "I saw Cynic a couple weeks back. She was out by Eltee. Didn't have a student then, but that might've changed. Think this boy of yours can handle Cynic?"

"She'll eat him for breakfast."

"What, wait?" Warrior looked between the two. "You're joking, right?"

Ash laughed. "Only if you keep that 'you allow girls' bullshit to yourself, kid. Cynic ain't got time for stupidity. She's been proving herself tougher than the boys since before you could walk."

Probably longer. Shade let his eyes sweep over Warrior as he squirmed. He didn't know Cynic personally, but he didn't need to ask her name, either. Shade kept track of every Night Rider's name, and Instance told him who Cynic was after he spent half past a week training her before setting her loose on the world.

Once, Cynic had been Bessia Servic, one of the rare female centurions in the Evendarian army. Women weren't *technically* prohibited from joining; tradition and custom simply discouraged them. A few did, anyway. Shade had known several, though he only knew Cynic by reputation.

She was one of the best, good enough to survive when the Northern Army fell to Olor early in the war, leading what was left of her legion in a guerrilla campaign that slowed the Olorian advance until the Southern Army got in position to engage them. They'd need people like her in the future...assuming she didn't get herself killed.

Then again, he could say the same for Ash. Vicious has potential.

Jury was still out on Warrior.

"Can I get you a little something after dinner, silver eyes?" A hand landed on Shade's left shoulder as the barmaid whispered in his ear.

Tension ripped through him like lightning. Shade's right hand immediately snapped back, fingers closing around the hilt of a dagger before conscious thought even flickered through his mind. It was halfway out of the scabbard before he stopped himself, stopped his right foot from shifting under his body so that he could twist left and stab *up*, catching the unsuspecting barmaid under the chin with the dagger.

"I could use a refill on the ale, honey." Ash's voice was deceptively friendly, but his eyes were on Shade's right hand. "And I might take you up on that desert."

Her hand lifted; Shade forced himself to relax. Ash, eyes on the barmaid, grinned.

She beamed. "I'm sure we could work something out, handsome."

"Oh, ew." Vicious made a face.

Shade eased his dagger back into its scabbard as the barmaid leaned in to take Ash's empty glass, popping a kiss on his cheek.

"Find me after," she whispered.

"Can I room with you?" Vicious turned to Warrior and Shade, her eyes pleading. "I'm not sharing with him if he's shacking up with her."

The barmaid and Ash both laughed. Shade let out a quiet breath and cursed his reflexes, pushing old memories down as hard as he could.

He would *not* think of that now. Not here.

The brand on the back of his neck burned.

Miles away, south of the Bridge, another Night Rider used the cover of darkness to their advantage. Bridgetown's square was quiet; Olorians viewed the evening as time to be spent with family, even those who tortured others for a living. It so happened that the Proctor of Bridgetown—the Olorian mayor—had two torturers in her employ. Both went home after leaving the body on display the day before.

No Evendarian would dare touch it, of course. Not after the display the Proctor's men put on. The townspeople had been forced to watch, as they always were when a Night Rider was tortured to death.

She arrived two days too late.

91

By now, the guards were growing lazy. They wanted to go home to their families, too, and they judged Bridgetown's Evendarians properly cowed. Tomorrow, they'd bully Evendarians into burying the body just to drive the sacrilege home. But tonight? Tonight was boring. One by one, the eight guards left until one remained alone.

He died with a knife buried in the back of his neck, never knowing what hit him. Cynic left his body for the Olorians to find; they'd bury him soon enough.

Instance was her concern. Dry-eyed, her movements made quick with fury, she cut him down and stole his body away. She burned him near dawn, miles away in the wilderness.

Then Cynic headed northeast, a plan forming in her mind.

17

CYNIC

Shade slept little that night, but he didn't expect to. Having both Vicious and Warrior in the room did not help; he spent most of the night staring at the ceiling, trying to stop memories from rolling through his mind. When that didn't work, he headed for the Blue Horse's bath, hoping to find it empty. Rhona kept the place pretty clean, and the water was usually at least lukewarm.

He'd wanted a hot bath for the past seven days, but at this point, Shade would settle for a cold one. Provided it was private. He was not in the mood to show his *other* scars off to strangers.

Unfortunately, there was an orgy in the bath. The Blue Horse was old enough to have both a cool and warm pool. Even in the wee hours of the morning, both overflowed with drinking bathers. Fortunately, Ash and his lady friend were not among them.

They were all Evendarians, though, which at least meant the participants all wanted to be there, and it really wasn't his business. He turned away before anyone could issue an invitation. That crowd looked far too welcoming, and the few glimpses he got made his skin crawl and brought up too many memories.

Sighing, Shade headed down to the stables, brushing Vic over and over again until morning came. Then he headed to the market and bought supplies enough to last a week, even with Warrior in tow.

Ash found him there, with both students in tow. "We're heading north. You going for the Bridge?"

"We are." It would be Shade's third crossing in ten days. What fun.

"May the Lady be with you, then. Try to avoid the weather." Ash held out a hand.

Shade shook it. "Ride well."

"Never forget." Ash's smile was lopsided. "C'mon, Vicious. Time to earn our keep."

Vicious laughed. Warrior frowned. "We get paid?"

"No. Mount up."

Reaching the Bridge took a full day; they camped at its head, arriving after dark. Warrior was a little more confident in the saddle by then, and the weather was calm, so Shade chose to press onward the next morning.

Crossing with a novice rider took most of the day. The main causeway was only thirty miles, but it was narrow even in good weather. Horses were sane creatures with more imagination than brains, and they didn't like not knowing what was under their feet.

Vic was an old Bridge hand, but even he didn't like unexpected waves. Warrior's mare bucked him off the first time a higher wave tickled her knees, leaving Shade to chase her down while Warrior, red-faced and soaked, dug sand out of unmentionable places. They walked the horses for a while after that, remounting when the ground was firmer.

Fortunately, Warrior was a fit kid. He rambled about working with his parents in the port and carrying sacks of this and that all day, so he kept up a decent pace.

"Aren't you tired?" Warrior asked as they remounted.

"Should I be?"

"I mean, you're, um, old." Warrior gulped. "Aren't you?"

Shade almost smiled. "Older than you, for certain."

At least twice as old, he didn't say. No use disabusing the boy of his assumptions; like most people, Warrior probably thought Shade older than he was. By some small miracle, Shade's black hair wasn't graying yet, but his weathered and scarred face made him look a decade greater than his actual age. It didn't help that he rarely smiled and found little joy in life.

He had too much to do for hope or joy.

Too much loss.

That night, they camped ten miles short of the foot of the Bridge while Warrior tried all too obviously not to complain. That turned into the Second Telling of Seril Rufio's Life Story, which Shade tried to tune out as best he could. By then, he was tired to the bone, and he *still* hadn't gotten a damn bath, which put him in a foul mood.

Add this to the list of reasons I don't take students. It tempts me to murder, he thought behind an expressionless face.

Under other circumstances, Shade would've pushed on to Bridgetown or Weltil—the former was larger, but Gunstrum's, in Weltil, was safer—but Warrior's mare wasn't up to another long day. Weltil had a decent horse market; that was reason enough to go there.

Once Warrior stopped trying to regale Shade with stories of climbing ships' rigging as a boy, sleep found both quickly.

Again, Shade dreamt of yellow eyes watching.

They reached Weltil an hour before noon, well-rested with the exception of Warrior's cranky mare, who tried to bite him when he mounted that morning.

"How do I give her up? Fanny was mater's." Warrior's blue eyes glistened suspiciously; Shade chose not to taunt him.

Cynic could do that, assuming she took the boy. If she didn't, Shade would find someone else before the boy's youth and optimism drove him insane. He had other things to do.

"A good horse can mean the difference between life and death out here. Fanny may have been a good horse once"—if Shade was being charitable—"but she's too old, now. Too slow."

"But—"

"Do you want to die out here?"

Warrior glowered. "No."

"Then cease arguing. We sell the horse and buy you a better one." Shade hated the way his accent came out when he got annoyed, and he stamped it down with a vengeance, digging up the rougher speech he'd learned years ago and used exclusively these days.

"Fine." Then Warrior perked up. "Do I get to pick the color? I'd like a black horse."

"We'll see."

Shade should've gotten rid of that damn mare back in Coelera. One of the *venatores'* horses would've been better than the aging and soon-to-be-lame Fanny, but they weren't really worthy of being a Night Rider's horse, either. If they had been, he'd have gotten a lot more than a hundred twenty-five sestertii for each of them.

Two hours later, they left the horse trader with Shade's purse four hundred sestertii lighter. A black gelding followed Warrior placidly. He wasn't the best horse in the bunch, but he was solid, brave, and fit—and unlikely to leave Warrior to die.

And the kid didn't shed a tear over Fanny, either. Good enough.

The same stableboy met them outside Gunstrum's stables, grinning when he spotted Shade accompanied by *two* horses.

"You and your friend kill those others dead?" he asked, displaying a full set of surprisingly clean teeth.

"Some of them." Thinking of Instance made Shade's throat tight.

"They were mean." The urchin scowled.

"Were they?"

"Yeah. Said we had to help them like they was the law. But no one Evendarian's the law these days. Everyone knows that." The boy laughed. "And Gunstrum told me that I should ignore them dick heads, anyway."

Warrior's jaw dropped. "Does your mater know you use words like that?"

The urchin shrugged. "She don't care. Olorians killed her years ago. Gunstrum took me in, and as long as I take care of them horses, I can say what I want."

Warrior's mouth opened and shut soundlessly. Shade chuckled.

"Come," he said, leading the way into Gunstrum's.

Gunstrum's had changed little in the seven days since Shade was last there. The formerly white paint and green on the outside still merged into a dingy green, but the atmosphere inside remained almost solely Evendarian. There was a nicer inn on the other side of Weltil, reserved for Olorian clientele who couldn't afford to stay in Bridgetown, so few bothered to come to Gunstrum's.

That was one reason Gunstrum's was one of Shade's favorite places.

He led Warrior to the bar, noting with relief that Alessa wasn't there. Deon, Gunstrum's nephew, was polishing glasses, and he looked up as they approached. "One room or two?"

"One." Much though Shade wished for privacy, he didn't dare leave Warrior on his own. "Two beds, if you have it."

"Room nine." Deon extended a key, which Shade slid inside his cloak.

Shade liked Deon. He never bothered with small talk and never told Alessa when Shade was around. Not that she wouldn't find out. The *hospitia* wasn't *that* big, and she lived on the top floor.

98

Suppressing the need to shudder, Shade gestured for Warrior to follow him up the stairs. Room nine was on the second floor and right over the patio awning. That made for an easy escape, if necessary—another reason Night Riders liked Gunstrum's so much.

The room was small, but it had two beds, a table, and a washbasin. The latrines were behind the main building, as were the kitchen and the bath. Maybe Shade would *finally* get his damned warm bath later, but after this long, he wasn't counting on it. Clearly, some god or another was against the idea.

They stayed in the room long enough to dump their saddlebags and bedrolls before heading back down to the dining room. Gunstrum met them on the stairs, his long face solemn.

"Rumor says Nydallas of Olor is in Polontis," he whispered. "Just thought you might want to know."

"Thank you." Shade filed that one away. Polontis was over a hundred miles away from Weltil along the Via Magus, but it was a curious destination for the Crown Prince of Olor.

Why not a city like Qelldoria, or even Bridgetown? Polontis was a decent-sized town, less rundown than Weltil, but no grand metropolis. Entertainment there was limited to a handful of theaters and a tiny circus, not enough to keep a famous hedonist entertained.

Polontis was more famous for its ties to Cirus, the Wizard's Haven. Cirus was nominally independent these days, under the rule of the Watcher—and the last scion of the Zhuid line was married to Nydallas. Rumor said there was little love between Annia Zhuid and Nydallas, and Shade wished them the utmost of misery.

To his right, Warrior was sheet white. "Isn't that the queen's eldest son?" he whispered.

"It is."

"Why's he out here?"

"Probably visiting his wife. Not our problem." Not yet, anyway. Shade led Warrior to the Night Riders' customary table, where Deon took their lunch orders.

Scowling, Shade ordered ale instead of the wine he wanted, but it was too early in the day to drink a bottle. And he needed to be sober if he was going to bathe.

"Do you usually run into other Night Riders on the road?" Warrior asked after ten minutes of blessed silence. The kid spent most of his time watching patrons trickle in; Gunstrum's main crowd came in the evening, but the gamblers started early, and two groups to the front right were deep into dice games.

"No."

"Oh." Warrior swallowed. "That seems lonely."

"I told you that this was a solitary life," Shade said. "Are you having second thoughts?"

"No. Of course not." Warrior's voice crackled a little, but he met Shade's gaze.

"Good."

It wouldn't be too late for Warrior to turn away for at least a month; by then, he'd be someone else's problem. Shade sure as hell wasn't going to slow his pace for that long, not with Nydallas nearby.

Don't think about that now.

Pushing aside memories—too many memories—took him a long moment, during which Shade stared at the bottom of his glass and ignored Warrior's people watching. He remembered

Nydallas too well, remembered his laugh, his cruelty, and his mother encouraging him.

Thinking about the pair of them made his brand itch, but he refused to touch it. Refused to give them that victory.

"Is that another Night Rider?" Warrior asked.

Shade's head snapped up. There was a figure framed in the doorway; red flashed as she removed her hood, revealing curly red hair not yet going gray that tried valiantly to escape a messy braid. Freckles framed hard blue eyes, and she moved like a broad-shouldered predator.

Gunstrum greeted her with a smile and gave her a drink, which she brought to their table. She stopped, towering over Shade and his companion.

"The legendary Shade, I presume," she said. "Your scars give you away."

"Cynic," he replied. "It's a pleasure."

Cynic's smile was cool. "It won't be once you hear what I have planned."

18

BRIDGETOWN

S hade sat back and studied her. "Unless it's my murder, you might be surprised."

Warrior squeaked out a gasp.

Cynic chuckled. "No." She sat down and sipped her drink, a dark ale that was one of Gunstrum's specialties. "Instance is dead. Killed four days ago in Bridgetown."

"Damn." Four days ago meant he led the *venatores* on a good chase; Shade last saw him two days before that. His throat felt tight.

"It was in the usual way. The proctor's torturers did their work for everyone to see." Cynic didn't twitch, but Warrior gagged on his ale. "Then they left his body on display until I stole it and burned it. He's at peace now."

"You did well."

"It was the least I could do. He was my mentor and my friend." Her eyes burned with hatred. "I want to avenge him."

"The people who caught him are already in the wind." Shade's chest was tight; he'd killed half the *venatores*, but damn it all if they weren't his countrymen. He hated the idea of hunting them

103

down almost as much as he hated the fact that they'd turned Instance over to Olorians in the first place.

"Those who killed him aren't."

"Are you talking about *assassination?*" Warrior whispered.

Cynic arched an eyebrow. "And who are you?"

"Warrior." He swallowed. "I think he wants you to mentor me."

"How charming. Do you have a problem with vengeance?"

"Um, should I?" Warrior glanced at Shade. "Do we do that? Is it murder?"

"Not when those who killed him are guilty of numerous other crimes against Evendarians—and will do so again if not stopped," Shade replied. He met Cynic's gaze. "You're determined to do this?"

"Yes, but I'm not stupid enough to do it alone. They'll expect that." She smiled. "Your reputation, on the other hand..."

"I would normally counsel you to wait." But Instance had died to protect Shade, to protect his secrets, and who was he to tell Cynic she should not avenge him? "But not today."

"Good. We'll leave in the morning."

Bridgetown was an easy day's ride away, along the aptly named Via Bridgefoot. Distracted by Cynic, Shade *still* didn't get his damned bath, but he figured he could do that once he got Warrior off his hands.

"You're not ready for this," Cynic told Warrior as they slowed. Bridgetown filled the horizon with the sun setting behind it. The air smelled of salt, even from here; Bridgetown was right on Fiskell Bay.

"Then what do I do?"

"You stay with the horses," Shade replied.

No need to mention that Vic and Cynic's horse wouldn't wander off; Warrior's new and still nameless gelding probably would. At least he was quicker than Fanny.

"You can also keep watch," Cynic said. Her tone was kinder than Shade's, although not by much. "That will help."

"All right." Warrior swallowed. "I still don't understand what you're doing, though. Not really."

"We're stopping someone who likes to hurt others. And who killed a Night Rider." Cynic's lips curled in fury.

Shade could stay silent. He was a man of many secrets: his identity, his ultimate goals, and even his friendships were not things he shared. Yet Cynic deserved to know the truth.

All Night Riders needed to.

"Instance was caught by Evendarians," he said. "They call themselves *venatores*, after the old government trappers. But they work for Olor."

She twisted in the saddle to stare. "They *what*?"

"I expect they turned him over to the Proctor." Shade pushed down his own anger, pushed down decades of knowing Instance—and knowing the man he'd been *before* he became a Night Rider, back before the war. "Eighteen of them chased me to Weltil. Instance and I met there; he was nailed with an arrow. We split up, and they caught him. The half that came after me, I killed."

He did not mention the young *venator* he left alive. Maybe the boy bled out. Maybe not. Either way, he certainly was seeking a career change.

Cynic's eyes narrowed. She was silent for several moments, like she was deciding who to blame. "Then you owe him."

"I do."

Evendar's criminal justice system had never been focused on prisons; criminals paid fines, were sentenced to hard labor, or—on rare occasions—were executed. Incarceration was a temporary thing, reserved only for those awaiting trial and considered a danger to those around them.

Olor's love of chains and imprisonment came as a rude surprise after the Fall. By now, thirteen years later, there was a prison in every town, as well as whipping posts in every forum. Torture was an accepted form of punishment in Olor, particularly for Evendarians, whom the law viewed as slaves. And some Olorian officials reveled in it.

Akhet vasAller, the Proctor of Bridgetown, was one of those. A minor member of the ruling family of Clas Aller, she was given Bridgetown as her private playground—and no one needed to tell Shade how she must have reveled in killing a Night Rider. Her reputation was dark. Evendarian slaves survived mere months in her employ; those who didn't die were sold, maimed, to the guilds that sold stress relieving or "pain" slaves.

Evendarian citizens of Bridgetown frequently fared just as badly. Rumor said anyone good-looking or capable enough wasn't permitted to leave the city, on pain of enslavement.

Bridgetown was a miserable city. Even slipping through it after dark made that apparent; there were too many echoing cries of pain and too many slaves chained outside doors for it to be anything else. Warrior opened his mouth to object as they passed a pair of scantily clad men being whipped, but Cynic shushed him.

Odds were that both those men had families who would suffer if they ran. And even if they didn't, getting both away from Bridgetown in a hurry would be troublesome. Cold fury crawled down Shade's spine at the thought of leaving them, at the thought of doing nothing, but they continued onwards, leading their horses between a pair of houses full of laughing Olorians at dinner.

"You have to choose your battles," he told Warrior when they were out of earshot. Most new Night Riders needed to hear that at least a half dozen times. This kid would be no exception.

"But aren't we supposed to save people?"

"They're already done." Cynic's voice was as cold as Shade felt, hollow and empty. She hissed out a breath. "I guarantee you that's not the first whipping those two have suffered. They'll survive."

"But—"

"No buts," Shade said. "You choose the fights you can win. You choose the ones that matter. We can stop that whipping, but then they'll know Night Riders are here, and we'll never get at the Proctor. And we might not be able to save them, not if they have families."

"Can't we save their families, too?"

Cynic snorted. "The Proctor's got hundreds of guards at her command. We can't fight them all, and if we start digging for too many people, they'll all come."

Warrior bit his lip. "Oh."

"Every action has consequences. You must learn to anticipate them if you're going to be a Night Rider," Shade said.

Cynic held up a hand, and they stopped. "This is where you stay," she said. "That's her house. The one behind the prison."

"Of course it is." Shade hadn't been to Bridgetown since years before the Fall, but he could recognize the old Prefect's villa, even with an ugly prison blocking his view.

"They say Akhet likes to listen to the screams." Cynic's face twisted into a snarl.

Shade smiled. "Let's test that theory."

19

CONSEQUENCES

Leaving their horses with Warrior, the two Night Riders slipped around the edge of the forum towards the prison and the Proctor's villa. Once, when home to the Prefect of Bridgetown, that villa had been an elegant and sweeping monument to Evendarian power and prestige. Now it was painted in blue and black, the colors of Clas Aller.

Olorian standards featuring Clas Aller's bull stood on either side of the main entryway, a reminder of Akhet vasAller's military service—hadn't she served in Fredirick vasGollep's army? Shade suppressed a smile. That made this even sweeter.

"She likes to tell people how she was one of the key officers at the Battle of the Bridge," Cynic hissed. "Said she got Bridgetown for her service there, but what everyone knows is that she's still sore over the injuries she took and likes to take them out on Evendarians."

"How barbaric."

"You'd think a good healing would set her straight, but apparently, the woman's a bitch." Cynic shrugged and then cocked her head to listen. "Is that what I think it is?"

Shade paused as they passed the prison. "I think so."

It wasn't screaming. No, whoever Akhet's torturers were working on was beyond screaming. Those were the quiet whimpers and labored breathing of someone in the throes of death, of a person pushed too far and reaching for darkness.

Shade knew those sounds too well, knew Instance made them just before he died. Far too many Evendarians had over the past twelve years... and would for years yet to come.

"Here first?" Cynic asked. "Might as well get those two monsters."

"Agreed." Silently, Shade drew his sword, comforted by the cool feel of her leather-covered grip in his hand.

Cynic did the same, drawing a dagger in her left hand. She was a tall woman, several inches taller than Shade's own average height, and made her schiavona look small.

They crept towards the prison doors. It was mid-November and nearly a new moon. There was very little moonlight but plenty of lamps and torches in the forum—less than there would have been under Evendarian rule, but enough that the pair danced from shadow to shadow.

Several long minutes passed before Shade could peer through the double-barred doors. There were two guards just inside, but both were looking in, not out, and the doors were not locked. Shade had broken into enough Olorian prisons to know what that meant. Someone important was inside.

He glanced at Cynic; she nodded, tiptoeing to the opposite side of the doors. Sneaking a quick glance at the hinges, Shade noted they were well-oiled. Good.

A quick push from his left hand sent the doors flying open; Shade leapt through them a split second later with Cynic on his heels. His silver-bladed schiavona snapped up, driving right through the throat of the lefthand guard, severing his throat and his vocal cords too quickly for him to scream. A split second later, Cynic killed the one on the right just as quietly, with a dagger to the base of the skull.

Both caught the dead bodies and lowered them to the ground.

By then, the whimpers had faded, but a light down the hallway to the right told Shade where the torturers were. Still, he paused for a moment to let his eyes adjust.

Olorian prisons were usually cramped and full, but the cells here were empty. *All of them.* There were multiple sets of chains in each and dark stains on the floor, but no prisoners. Stalking towards the light, Shade double-checked every cell along the way.

All empty.

What kind of operation *was* Akhet vasAller running in this city?

The last room on the right was the standard location for a torture chamber; Olorian prisons usually had one on each end, and the left end was dark and quiet. But voices drifted out of this one through a partway open door—why close it and shut the sounds of terror and pain away?

Fury rose again; Shade forced it down. To his side, he could see Cynic's pale face pinched and tight. She was having a harder time containing her anger, and her knuckles were white where she gripped her weapons. But her hands were steady.

Let's kill these assholes, she mouthed.

Shade didn't bother with an answer; he just shoved this door open, too, but this time he let Cynic lead into the room. She cut right; he went left, each surprising and killing a guard within seconds. Much to Shade's surprise, there was a second set of guards, these flanking Akhet vasAller herself.

And here Shade had thought they'd have to hunt her down. How convenient.

"Kill them!" The Proctor wasn't armed and backed away while her guards advanced.

Cynic's thrown dagger took the first down; Shade stepped forward, parried a wild thrust, and stabbed the second in the heart. He landed in a heap as Akhet scurried behind the two torturers, ignoring the dead body on the floor.

The dead woman was Evendarian, of course. Shade didn't need more than a glance to know that or to know she was dead. Her guts decorated the floor, as well as one torturer's hands.

One torturer reached for a dead guard's sword, only for Cynic to kick him in the face and take his head off with a powerful downward slash. Shade's kill was more economical; when the other torturer tried to run, Shade simply caught him by the arm and drove his schiavona into the base of his neck. Momentum carried it down and severed his spine and several other vital organs. By the time Shade twisted the blade free, the torturer was already dead.

"I can pay you. Don't kill me. I can give you whatever you want." Akhet held her hands up, backing into the far wall.

"Can you bring Instance back to life?" Cynic stalked forward.

Akhet blinked. "Who?"

"The Night Rider your monsters killed!"

"I was just doing my duty!" Akhet shrank back, her voice rising to a quiet scream. "It's not my fault. And I can pay you. All you have to do is leave. I won't tell anyone, I swear."

Cynic stopped. Spat. "Coward. You disgust me."

"*Please!* I don't want to die."

"Neither did Instance, but I bet you gave him a bunch of choices, didn't you?" Cynic leaned in close. "Did you offer him mercy, or did you ask them to draw it out for your *entertainment*?"

"Stop playing with her and end it, Cynic," Shade said.

He was counting seconds in his head, estimating how long it would take for Akhet's soldiers to reach them from the guardhouse. They had time—not enough to burn the poor Evendarian woman Akhet had tortured to death—but not if Cynic continued taunting the Proctor.

Tormenting an enemy was not the Night Rider way, either.

Cynic twisted to glare at him, and for a moment, he thought she would argue. Instead, she turned back to Akhet and whipped her sword across the Proctor's throat.

Akhet collapsed in a heap.

They moved out and met up with Warrior without another word, slipping out of the city before Akhet's guards could track them.

20

FINALLY

"Are you sure you don't want to ride with us for a little while? We make a good team," Cynic said the next morning.

"Thank you, but no. I prefer to ride alone."

"Why?" Warrior rose from checking his gelding's hooves, looking stiff. The kid still wasn't used to sleeping in a rough camp under the stars, but he was putting in a good effort. "You didn't get Cynic killed."

"Let's just say that my charming personality is best suffered in small doses," Shade replied.

Cynic laughed; Warrior just shrugged. "I don't think you're that bad."

"I have other things to do, and you have lessons to learn. Cynic will teach you well." The part of Shade that had once been a man with social skills knew he should be touched by Warrior's kindliness, but he just couldn't.

Teaching Warrior was exhausting. He needed to get rid of him before Shade snapped and said something that broke the kid. Shade needed *space*, too.

And maybe he could finally take that god's forsaken bath.

"Ride well." Cynic held out a hand.

He took it. "Never forget."

Shade mounted Vic and rode away without looking back.

His first stop was Gunstrum's, again. The *hospitia* was quiet when he walked into the dining room to find Gunstrum polishing the bar. Halfway into the afternoon was usually a lull before the dinner rush, which was exactly what Shade was hoping for.

"Is your hot water working?" Shade asked by way of greeting.

Gunstrum blinked. "Aye."

"How much for an hour's guaranteed privacy in your bath? I'll require the key."

"For you? Free." Gunstrum smiled. "It's empty now. Deon just cleaned it."

Shade dug into his purse and pulled a silver denarius out by feel. He dropped it on the bar, meeting Gunstrum's eyes when the barkeep opened his mouth to argue. It closed with an audible click.

"The key, if you please. A room, also."

Even a single silver denarius was grossly overpaying for a private bath, a room, and as many meals as Shade could want. One denarius was worth a thousand sestertii, enough to buy two acres of decent land back when Evendar was owned by Evendarians.

But Shade always overpaid. Firstly, because he took money off dead Olorians who didn't need it and gave it to Evendarians who did. Secondly, because people flush with money were less bribable, and thus less likely to betray him.

Not that he thought Gunstrum would betray him. But paranoia had kept him alive this long, and Shade liked breathing.

Gunstrum stared at the coin for a moment before pocketing it. One silver denarii would keep the *hospitia* running for weeks. "Room nine again, all right?"

"Perfect."

Shade accepted both keys, nodded, and headed up the stairs. After a quick look around the room—paranoia, again—he dropped his saddlebags, cloak, and bedroll off. Grabbing clean clothes, he headed towards the bath, out behind the main building.

Gunstrum's, like most private bathhouses, only had one bath. Fortunately, it was a hot one. Shade put down his sword in easy reach of the bath's edge, then moved to the side and started divesting himself of the various throwing knives and daggers hidden in his boots, belt, and clothing. These he lined up neatly on the bench, checking their edges and noting which needed sharpening.

He could do that later.

Next, he peeled off his tunic, undertunic, belt, trousers, boots, and undergarments. All smelled ripe and needed washing; hopefully, he could get that done before he left. Night Riders couldn't afford to carry too many sets of clothing, but damn, he missed the days when he could bathe and change regularly.

He snorted. Better to dwell on missing freedom or home. Either was as useful as mourning for clean clothes.

Finally, Shade slipped into the bath, closing his eyes and letting himself relax for the first time in too long. The hot water was good for sore muscles and old injuries, good at easing the stress knots out. Unfortunately, it was not good at quieting his mind.

He'd have a good meal tonight and start early. Then it was a hundred-mile ride to Polontis and a certain Olorian prince.

Today was the twenty-fifth of November. Even an easy ride would let him arrive by the twenty-eighth, the eighth anniversary of King Valhin II Noyce's death. That conceited princeling had killed Evendar's last king and boasted of it regularly.

Shade would make sure he paid for it.

FINIS

Thank you very much for taking the time to read this novella! I hope you enjoyed it! As an indie author, I treasure each and every one of my readers. If you would be so kind as to leave a review, it would mean the world to me!

Afterword

Shade finally got his bath, but he still has to catch the prince.

Shade's story - and his hunt for Prince Nydallas - continues *in* Night Rider, *currently on Kindle Vella.* Kindle Vella is Amazon's serial reading platform, where you can read stories one episode at a time. It's great for people who have limited time (like me!) and need to catch a chapter at lunch, between meetings, or before bed. But you an also binge read on Vella, where *Night Rider* is an ongoing story full of twists, turns, and great characters.

Evendar is a broken nation. What little hope her people have comes from Night Riders like Shade...and from a secret Underground rebellion in the heart of the capital city itself. In *Night Rider*, we'll meet three other unlikely heroes who, along with Shade, will change Evendar's very future. An epic fantasy in the tradition of *Game of Thrones* and *The Lord of the Rings, Night Rider* is for those who like their stories complicated, their characters gray, and yet want hope to remain.

Come on over to Vella and give *Night Rider* a try.

NIGHT RIDER

A STORY OF THE LEGACY

R.G. ROBERTS

About R.G. Roberts

R.G. Roberts is a veteran of the U.S. Navy, currently living in Connecticut and working as a Manufacturing Manager for a major medical device manufacturer. While an officer in the Navy, R.G. Roberts served on three ships, taught at the Surface Warfare Officer's School, and graduated from the U.S. Naval War College with a masters degree in Strategic Studies & National Security, with a concentration in leadership.

She is a multi-genre author, and has published in military thrillers, science fiction, epic fantasy, and alternate history. She rode horses until she joined the Navy (ships aren't very compatible with high-strung jumpers) and fenced (with swords!) in college. Add in the military experience and history degree, and you get A+ anatomy for a fantasy author. However, since she also enjoyed her time in the Navy and loves history, you'll find her in those genres as well.

You can find R.G. Roberts' website at www.rgrobertswriter.com or find all her links at linktr.ee/rgroberts. From there, you can join her newsletters! Joining the newsletter will get you a free novella, set in either the War of the Submarine or World of the Legacy universes (or both, if you like both genres). Newsletters are a twice-a-month affair, so there won't be a ton of spam in your inbox, but you'll be the first to hear about sales, get sneak peeks of new writing, and get to read a few subscriber-only short stories, too!

Also By

War of the Submarine

Before the Storm (novella)

Cardinal Virtues
The War No One Wanted (coming soon)
Read the serial version of *War of the Submarine* on
Kindle Vella and get to start *The War No One Wanted*
before anyone else!

War of the Submarine Shorts
Never Take a Recon Marine to a Casino Robbery
(subscriber exclusive)

Stories of the Legacy

Shade (novella)
Shadow (coming soon)

Night Rider

Legacy Shorts:
Prelude to Conquest (subscriber exclusive)
The First Ride (subscriber exclusive)
City of Light (Street Team exclusive)

Alternate History

Against the Wind

Caesar's Command

Short Stories

Agent of Change
Once Upon a Dragon (coming soon!)

Made in the USA
Coppell, TX
06 August 2025

52816081R00075